———————————— ★ ————————————

"Good thing we had us a little rain here last week," Grice said when Rhodes shone his light on the body.

"Otherwise he'd likely have burned up my whole pasture. What do you think'd make a fella blow up like that?"

Rhodes said he didn't know.

"Smells terrible, too," Grice said. "Sort of like a barbecue, but off a little if you know what I mean."

Rhodes knew. He felt a little sick at his stomach. He'd seen dead men before, but never one who'd been burned so badly.

"Made a pretty considerable noise when he blew up," Grice said. He didn't seem too bothered by the smell. "You ever hear of a fella blowin' up like that before?"

Rhodes never had, and it was not until the next day that he figured out what had actually happened. He had found the remains of a gasoline can near the scene.

———————————— ★ ————————————

BILL
CRIDER

DEATH BY
ACCIDENT

WORLDWIDE®

TORONTO • NEW YORK • LONDON
AMSTERDAM • PARIS • SYDNEY • HAMBURG
STOCKHOLM • ATHENS • TOKYO • MILAN
MADRID • WARSAW • BUDAPEST • AUCKLAND

This book is dedictaed to the memory
of Ellen Nehr and Barry Gardner

DEATH BY ACCIDENT

A Worldwide Mystery/March 2000

First published by St. Martin's Press, Incorporated.

ISBN 0-373-26343-0

Visit us at www.worldwidemystery.com

Printed in U.S.A.

DEATH BY ACCIDENT

ONE

THE CLEARVIEW Sons and Daughters of Texas had put a lot of time and money into improving the Old Settlers' Grounds since Sheriff Dan Rhodes had been there a year or so earlier. His visit this time wasn't going to be any more pleasant than the last one, however, if the phone call Hack Jensen had told him about was any indication.

Rhodes drove onto the grounds through an arched gateway that no longer leaned precariously to one side. The name of the campground had been freshly painted in black letters on the span of the arch. Rhodes could see bright new wood on the dance pavilion, too. All the rotted boards had been replaced in the floor, roof, and steps. The sides had been straightened and braced.

Years ago Rhodes had square-danced on the pavilion with girls who were grown up now and married, with children older than they themselves had been on those summer nights when they had gone allemande left and do-si-do. Some of the women still lived in town, though most of them were long gone from Clearview. Rhodes had heard that one of them was a dean at a community college and that another was a social worker somewhere near Dallas. He wondered if they ever thought about the square dances or the Old Settlers' Grounds. He figured they probably didn't.

Rhodes drove the county car past the old pavilion on a road covered in fresh white gravel, another recent improvement if you didn't mind a little dust. He stopped his car by Ty Berry's blue Ford pickup and got out.

The day was warm, and the sun was high in a blue sky flecked with only a few high clouds, but it was November and there was a not-so-subtle hint of fall in the air. Rhodes wasn't sure just what it was. It could have been the angle of the sunlight through the high tree limbs, the light breeze that swished through the red and yellow leaves, or just the smell of things, as if some faint scent of the high country was sneaking in on the breeze.

Rhodes started off on the path toward the two old swimming pools that had been built down by the river. Long ago, when the citizens of Blacklin County had devoted a full week every summer to celebrating the contributions of the county's original settlers, the Grounds had been filled for days with laughing people. There had been playgrounds for the children, and the swimming pools had been popular spots for cooling off.

But the yearly celebrations had stopped even before Rhodes was a boy. There was no evidence remaining of seesaws or swings, and the pools had become dangerous. Their concrete sides had cracked, and chunks had broken off and settled on the bottom. The river still flowed nearby and still fed water to the pools, but no one was supposed to swim in them any more. People did occasionally, but it was a risky business, if not exactly against the law.

It was cool in the shade of the pecan trees, and Rhodes heard a squirrel scampering through the branches. A pecan fell from above, missing Rhodes by not more than a couple of feet. He wasn't sure whether it had been dropped, dislodged, or deliberately aimed in his direction. You never could tell about squirrels.

Rhodes looked over toward what was left of the Wishing Well. He had thrown a penny or two into that well when he was a kid, but he couldn't remember what he had wished for. Whatever it had been, it hadn't been what he had found there a year ago.

Rhodes went on down the path, dry leaves crackling under his feet. Turning a bend and looking down the steep bank, he saw Ty Berry standing by one of the swimming pools.

Berry was the president of the Clearview Sons and Daughters of Texas. He was short and thin, and he'd drawn his eyebrows together so often in perpetual worry that some precious bit of Blacklin County history was going to be destroyed or forgotten that there was a permanent line running up from the bridge of his nose. He had been the driving force behind the restoration of the Old Settlers' Grounds, and he had personally raised nearly every penny of the money that had been spent on the project.

He had both hands thrust into the pockets of the

blue nylon jacket he was wearing. A Clearview Cat-amounts baseball cap covered his balding head, and he was pacing nervously up and down the edge of the pool.

The water in the pool was as clear and green as Rhodes remembered having ever seen it. Leaves floated on the surface and covered the bottom, but they had fallen only recently and Rhodes could see no dirt or slime.

The Sons and Daughters had spent quite a bit of their money in cleaning the pools and removing the debris of years from them. They hadn't repaired the cracks, and they hadn't made the pools safe for swimming. There hadn't been enough money for that, and the pools were so far out of town that re-pairing them wouldn't have been advisable. It would just have encouraged unsupervised swimming. But the Sons and Daughters had certainly made the pools look better.

The sunlight filtered through the tree branches and the dying leaves and sparkled off the water, and somewhere high above, a bird, either a year-round resident or one that hadn't yet left for a warmer climate farther south, whistled softly. In the river, three turtles sitting on a log seemed to sense Rhodes's presence at the same instant, and all three slipped into the smooth green water, hardly rippling its surface.

Rhodes thought it was a peaceful and relaxing scene, except for one thing: the dead body that floated in the nearer pool, only a few feet from where Ty Berry was standing next to a bright red and white sign that read:

DANGER!
ABSOLUTELY NO SWIMMING!
THE WATER IN THIS POOL COULD BE
POLLUTED!
NO LIFEGUARD ON DUTY!
DANGER!

Berry looked up, saw Rhodes, and pulled his right hand out of his jacket pocket to wave. Rhodes waved back and walked down the crumbling concrete steps to the pool.

"I called the ambulance, too," Berry said. "I guess you beat them here."

"I was in the neighborhood," Rhodes said.

TWO

RHODES HAD BEEN on his way back to Clearview after driving to Thurston to check on a welding machine that had been abandoned on a county road. The man who'd called in about the welding machine wanted to know if he could keep it if no one claimed it, and Rhodes had been forced to disappoint him. The machine had been reported stolen in a neighboring county the previous evening, along with the truck that the owner had used to transport it. The welding machine was in a ditch by the side of the road, but there had been no sign of the truck.

"Any idea who that is?" Rhodes asked, looking down at the body, which was floating facedown.

"I haven't tried to get a look," Berry said. "He . . . he was at the bottom of the pool, but I pulled him up. I don't know why I did it."

Berry looked a little queasy, and Rhodes didn't blame him. It wasn't every day that you found a dead man, much less one that had been in the water for a while.

"After I pulled him up, he sort of floated," Berry said. "I didn't do anything else. I thought you'd want me to leave things pretty much like I found them."

Rhodes nodded. "You were right."

His knees cracked as he knelt down to look at the

body, which had sunk back under the water about six inches. It was that of a man who had been wearing only a pair of jockey shorts, and it was tangled in a practically new rope, one end of which was tied to a dead-looking tree limb that floated several feet away in the pool. The rope that wasn't twisted around the body had absorbed enough water to sink, but it hadn't pulled the limb under.

"Looks like he was swinging over the water on that rope," Berry said. "The limb broke, and he fell in and drowned. Maybe the limb hit him on the head. And he was probably drunk."

"Why do you say that?" Rhodes asked.

"Why else would he be swimming out here at this time of the year? That water's cold!" Berry jammed his right hand back into his jacket pocket and shook his head. "And it's dangerous to swim alone, here or anywhere. Do you think he couldn't read the sign?"

Berry took a step and whacked the red-and-white warning sign with his hand.

"Do you think it wasn't big enough for him to see? Or do you think he even looked at it?"

"He probably just ignored it," Rhodes said.

"That's right," Berry said. "He ignored it, and now he's dead. I tried to tell everyone that this would happen if we cleaned up the pools. I tried to get them to agree to drain them, but would they listen to me? Hell, no."

He stalked away and stood looking angrily out over the pool. "And now what's going to happen?" He didn't wait for Rhodes to answer. "I'll tell you what's going to happen. First of all, everybody'll blame the Sons and Daughters for this. They'll say that we should've built a fence around the pool or something stupid like that. Never mind that the pools've been here for ninety years without anybody drowning in them. And then somebody'll sue us, sign or no sign."

The breeze shook brown leaves out of the pecan trees, and they spiraled down toward the water. Rhodes stood up. His knees cracked again. He wished they wouldn't do that.

"You know what Bob Dylan said in the sixties?" Berry asked.

Rhodes remembered quite a few things that Bob Dylan had said, but he didn't know which one of them Berry was referring to.

"Hey, Mr. Tambourine Man?" Rhodes guessed.

Berry shook his head. "He said that everybody must get stoned. Remember?"

Rhodes said that he remembered.

"I thought you would. But he wouldn't say that these days. You know what he'd say?"

Rhodes looked down at the body and shook his head.

"He'd say everybody must get sued," Berry told him.

"Maybe no one will sue. There was a warning sign here, after all."

Berry laughed, but it wasn't a happy sound. "That woman sued McDonald's when she spilled the coffee in her lap, didn't she? Surely you read about that. You'd think anyone would know coffee was hot, but she got a judgment for millions. Oh, we'll get sued, all right.''

Rhodes decided that he might as well agree. ''Maybe so. But that doesn't really matter right now. What matters is that we've got a dead man here. Any idea where his clothes are?''

''Right over there,'' Berry said, pointing to where the bath house had once stood. Only part of the foundation remained. ''Behind that tree.''

Rhodes walked over to the tree Berry had indicated. Sure enough, the clothes were there—a pair of faded Wrangler jeans, a pair of cheap roping boots, a western shirt, socks, a belt with a buckle the size of a hubcap, and a T-shirt that had been white at one time but now had a distinct yellowish tinge. Nothing was folded. It was as if everything had simply been tossed there as someone undressed.

He looked back at Berry. ''Any idea where that rope was tied?''

''In one of those trees close to you, I guess,'' Berry said.

Rhodes looked around. There were several pecan trees towering over him. All of them had limbs that stretched out over the pool.

''You could run along the bank there,'' Berry said. ''Then you could grab the rope and keep right on going, swing out over the water, and drop straight down and in. Not a good thing to do if you're drunk, though, but of course a jury won't consider that. They'll just award the family eighty million dollars and go home to watch themselves on TV.''

Rhodes didn't think it was worth mentioning that

Blacklin County had never had a trial that merited television coverage and wasn't likely to. He didn't think Berry would be comforted.

"You seem mighty worried about a lawsuit," he said.

"Hell, yes. Wouldn't you be?"

"I'm more worried that a man's dead here."

"Through his own damn fault. If he'd stayed home and stayed sober, he'd still be alive."

Rhodes wasn't so sure about that. Several things were bothering him. For one, it didn't seem likely that anybody, drunk or sober, would suddenly decide to go to the Old Settlers' Grounds for a swim all by himself, much less decide to go for a swim where no one had been accustomed to swimming for fifty years or more. How had he gotten here, anyway? And where had that rope come from?

"Did you see his car?" Rhodes asked.

Berry walked over to where Rhodes was standing under the tree. "Yeah. That's why I came down to the pool. I was out here checking on the Burleson cabin. There's a pickup parked behind it, little Chevy S-10. I looked around, but I didn't see anybody, so I came down here. That's when I found him and called the jail."

"How'd you call?"

Berry pulled a cellular phone out of his pocket and held it up without saying anything. Then he put it back.

"Do you come out here often?" Rhodes asked.

"At least once a week. I have to check on the Burleson cabin, like I said."

The Burleson cabin was the central issue in a feud between the Sons and Daughters and another organization, the Clearview Historical Society. The Society claimed that the cabin, supposedly the oldest structure in the county and supposedly built by Cletus Burleson, one of the very first settlers, had been moved from near Clearview to the Old Settlers' Grounds in the early part of the century.

The Society members, prodded by Faye Knape, their president, wanted the cabin brought back to Clearview and set up on the grounds of the county courthouse where they thought it belonged and where they hoped it might be more of a tourist attraction than it was hidden off in the country. The Sons and Daughters believed that if they didn't keep a close watch, the Society would sneak out to the Grounds in the dead of night to spirit the cabin away.

"Do you look around the Grounds every time you're here?" Rhodes asked.

"Every time. We've put a lot of work into this place, and we're going to revive the Old Settlers' Days celebration next summer. We want to be sure everything's in top shape."

"Did you ever see a rope hanging from one of these trees?"

Berry looked over his shoulder at the body, then back at Rhodes. "What if I did?"

Uh-oh, Rhodes thought. No wonder Berry was worried about a lawsuit. He'd known the rope was there and hadn't done anything about it.

"If you did," he said, "it might mean that someone had been swimming here before. You should have reported it, or taken it down.''

"It was just a rope in a tree," Berry said. "I didn't think anything about it."

Maybe, Rhodes thought, but more likely Berry just hadn't thought it was worth fooling with. And certainly he hadn't thought anyone would drown.

Rhodes looked at the jeans on the ground. There was a bulge in the right-hand back pocket, and Rhodes reached down to take out the billfold. He flipped it open to look at the driver's license in its clear plastic holder.

"Peter Yeldell," he said. "You know him?"

Berry shook his head. "Heard of him. Never met him, though. You?"

Rhodes nodded. He'd heard of Peter Yeldell, all right. Better known as Pep, Yeldell had been in trouble for most of his thirty-one years. Little things, usually. Joyriding and minor in possession of alcohol when he was a kid, DWI, abusive language, and assault when he got a little older. Rhodes had arrested him once or twice, and the deputies a lot more than that.

"I hear something up there," Berry said, looking up toward the road. "Somebody's coming."

Rhodes stuck the billfold back in the jeans. "That would be the ambulance," he said.

THREE

RHODES SENT BERRY up the hill to keep the ambulance away. He didn't want anyone else down there while he was investigating the crime scene.

But it hadn't been the ambulance that they'd heard. It was Ruth Grady, one of the deputies. She was short and stout and utterly dependable.

"Hack gave me a call," she said as she came down the hill. "He thought you might need some help with the crime scene."

"He was right," Rhodes said, glad that Hack had made the call. Hack hadn't taken to the idea of a woman deputy at first, but Ruth had won him over quickly. "Where's Berry?"

"I told him to stay up there, wait for the ambulance," Ruth said. She looked at the floating body. "Anybody we know?"

"Pep Yeldell," Rhodes told her. "You've brought him in a time or two."

Ruth nodded. "I sure have. Mostly for drunk and disorderly. What do you think happened here?"

"It looks like an accident. Pep got drunk, decided to come for a swim, and took a swing over the water on that rope. The limb broke, and he drowned."

"You think the limb hit him on the head?"

"That's one of the things we'll have Dr. White check," Rhodes said. White did the autopsies for the county, saving a lot of money and time that would have been wasted if the body had to be sent to Dallas or Waco.

Ruth bent down to get a better look at the rope. "Yeldell was alone?"

"That's what it looks like. His truck's up there behind the Burleson cabin. We'll check it later."

They photographed the scene, then searched the area around the pool thoroughly and found nothing, not even so much as a beer can. Rhodes wondered about that and then remembered that Ty Berry came out every week. He probably policed the area each time. There was nothing at all to indicate that there had been anyone with Yeldell.

"Let's check out the truck," Rhodes said at last. "Maybe there's something there."

"Better take that rope with us," Ruth said.

Rhodes agreed, and he knelt down by the side of the pool to unwind the rope from Yeldell's body.

"I wonder how he got so tangled up," he said.

"He might have twisted around in the air when the limb broke," Ruth said.

"I guess we'll take the limb, too," Rhodes said. "We might need it later."

He stood up and pulled the freed rope toward him hand over hand, looping it as he gathered it in. The limb coasted over the top of the water, making ripples that spread across the pool and slapped gently against the concrete. When the limb got almost to the edge of the pool, Rhodes bent down and picked it up.

"Ready?" Ruth said.

Rhodes hefted the waterlogged rope and the tree limb. "Let's go."

They climbed the hill to where Ty Berry waited by the ambulance, which had arrived while Rhodes and Ruth were doing the crime scene. Rhodes stopped to talk, Ruth went on toward the Burleson cabin.

"Find anything?" Berry asked, looking at the rope and limb that Rhodes carried.

"No," Rhodes said. "This is just the stuff we already knew about."

He put the rope and limb in the trunk of the county car and then told the ambulance attendants that it was all right for them to get the body.

"Take it to Ballinger's Funeral Home, and tell Clyde to give Dr. White a call."

One of the attendants nodded, and they went down the hill.

"Is there any need for me to stay around here?" Berry asked.

Rhodes told him that there wasn't.

"I guess I'll go on back to town, then. See about a lawyer. Get ready for the lawsuit."

"Let's hope there won't be one," Rhodes said.

"If the family doesn't bring one, Faye Knape probably will," Berry said. "I wouldn't be surprised if she were behind this whole thing."

"Do you think she had something to do with Yeldell's death?" Rhodes asked.

"No, no. Nothing like that. She wouldn't have had anything to do with it directly. But who put that rope up there in that tree? Think about it. It was on a dead limb. She'd know that someone would be sure to try a swing on it, and if they didn't get killed, they might get hurt. I wouldn't put it past her to have put that rope there.''

It sounded pretty far-fetched to Rhodes, and he said so. For one thing, he couldn't imagine Faye Knape climbing a tree.

''You don't know that woman if you think she wouldn't do it,'' Berry said. ''She's a maniac.''

Rhodes knew that Faye Knape was obsessive about the history of Clearview, but he didn't think she was a maniac.

''She's just a little eccentric,'' he said.

''Hah. I'll bet she's mixed up in this. You'll see.''

''If she is, I'll find out,'' Rhodes said, but Berry didn't hear him. He was already on his way to his truck.

THE BURLESON CABIN didn't look like anything special. It sat up on blocks sawed from some kind of tree trunk, and it was made of hand-hewn logs that had weathered to a light gray color over the years. The mortar that had been used to fill the cracks was mostly gone. There had been a chimney at one time, but it had long since disappeared. The hole in the wall had been boarded up sometime in the past. There was no glass in the windows, and most of the rough wood shingles were missing from the roof.

Rhodes walked around to the back, where Ruth was looking around a blue Chevy S-10. He rustled through ankle-deep leaves that had fallen from a huge burr oak tree.

"Find anything?" Rhodes asked.

"Not a thing. Maybe we should vacuum these leaves."

"I don't think we have to," Rhodes said. "If there had been another car in here, it would be easy to tell."

Yeldell's truck had crushed a path through the leaves, but there was no sign that another vehicle had been there.

"Anything in the truck?" Rhodes asked.

"A couple of cardboard beer cartons. Lots of empties in the bed of the truck."

It was about what Rhodes had figured.

"You know what worries me about this?" Ruth asked.

"That it looks like an accident," Rhodes said. "And that makes one too many accidents around here lately."

"That's right," Ruth said.

"But the two accidents don't have anything in common," Rhodes said. "This one's a drowning."

"That's different from the other one, all right," Ruth said.

Rhodes nodded. In the other one, a man had exploded.

FOUR

THE MAN WAS John West, and he had exploded a little more than two weeks earlier on a county road outside of Clearview at around 2:00 a.m.

"Two-oh-three exactly," David Grice had told Rhodes. "I put my glasses on and looked at that little digital clock I got at Wal-Mart's when I heard him blow up, and I called your office right after that."

Hack had taken the call and phoned Rhodes, who drove to the scene. West's clothes had burned away, and his body was a blackened mass. The grass in the bar ditch had burned in a circle around him.

Grice, who lived in a farmhouse a few hundred yards down the road, had been waiting by the ditch when Rhodes arrived.

"Good thing we had us a little rain here last week," Grice said when Rhodes shined his light on the body. "Otherwise, he'd likely have burned up my whole pasture. What do you think'd make a fella blow up like that?"

Rhodes said that he didn't know.

"Smells terrible, too," Grice said. "Sort of like a barbecue, but off a little if you know what I mean."

Rhodes knew. He felt a little sick at his stomach.

He'd seen dead men before, but never one who'd been burned so badly.

"Made a pretty considerable noise when he blew up," Grice said. He didn't seem too bothered by the smell. "Course I had the window up a little crack, couple or three inches. I like to get a little air in the room, even if it is the fall of the year. That's why I heard him, I guess. You ever hear of a fella blowin' up like that before?"

Rhodes never had, and it was not until the next day that he figured out what had actually happened. He had found the remains of a gasoline can near the scene.

Ruth Grady had been with him that time, too.

"So you think a car hit him while he was carrying the gas can?" she asked.

"That's right," Rhodes said. "It hit the can first, probably, then him. When the can burst, a spark from the metal must have set off the explosion. The gas got all over West, and he burned up. The impact of the crash is what killed him, though."

By that time they had identified the body. It was easy after they got a call from West's wife to say that he was missing.

But what West's wife hadn't been able to tell them was where West had been and why he was carrying a gas can.

"Obviously his car had run out of gas," Ruth said.

"That's the logical answer," Rhodes said. "But where's his car?"

They had searched both sides of the road several

miles, more than the distance West was likely to have walked, but there was no car to be found.

"What about the car that hit him?" Ruth asked. "Surely it was damaged."

Rhodes agreed that it must have been. "If we see it, we'll know it. And maybe it'll be taken to a body shop. I'll put out the word for anyone who sees it to give us a call."

But there hadn't been any calls, and the investigation seemed to have reached a dead end. According to his wife, Kara, and the family's friends, West had no enemies and no reason to be out on a country road alone late at night with a gas can in his hand.

Rhodes had questioned West's wife at length, but she could tell him nothing more than the fact that West hadn't come home from work. He often worked late at the little auto parts store he owned, she said, because he had trouble finding reliable help and had to keep the books and do all the restocking and inventory himself, after he'd closed the doors for the day.

It hadn't taken Rhodes long to find out that West didn't have any trouble at all finding reliable help, or at least help that he trusted to take care of things at the store. A young man named Jerry Tate did most of the things West's wife believed West was doing after hours, while West took off for an evening of drinking with his friends.

Tate had one of the flattest flattop haircuts Rhodes had seen since he was about twelve years old. He imagined you could have set a glass of water on the top of Tate's hair and it wouldn't wobble.

Tate said that he didn't know where West went after work, and he didn't care.

"He pays me to work in the store, and that's what I do," Tate told the sheriff. "So that's what I do—I work in the store, and I don't ask any questions about where he goes after he leaves here. He pays me overtime to stay and get all the ducks in a row, and I'm glad to do it. The only reason I know where he goes is that somebody told me about seeing him at some club one night."

"Who told you that?"

"I don't remember," Tate said, and Rhodes could see that he wasn't going to get any more out of him.

It didn't really matter. Knowing West's habit, Rhodes was able to find out in only a few hours that West liked to hang around with his brother, Tuffy. Tuffy drove a wrecker and owned a wrecking yard on the outskirts of Clearview. He spent a lot of his time in places like The County Line, a honky-tonk that Rhodes knew only too well, thanks to his recent investigation of the murder of one of Clearview High's assistant football coaches.

Tuffy hadn't been any help when Rhodes asked about his brother. Rhodes drove out to the wrecking yard to talk to him. The yard was surrounded by a high sheet-metal fence that had rusted badly, and it was filled with the bodies of wrecked cars, jumbled together as if the yard had been the scene of a gigantic destruction derby. Some of them had rusted as badly as the fence.

Occasionally a car crusher would come by and flatten some of the wrecks like cards in a deck, after which they would be stacked on a trailer and hauled away.

Tuffy met Rhodes outside the door of the sheet-metal building that served as both an office and a parts department. John sold new parts, and Tuffy sold used ones.

"I don't know a thing about what John was doing that night," he told Rhodes. "We had a couple of beers at The County Line, talked about the football team a little, and then he left."

He paused and gave Rhodes a significant look. "I thought our boys were on their way to state, but I guess that's all over with."

It wasn't exactly Rhodes's fault that the Clearview Catamounts hadn't won their play-off game after the coach's murder, but a lot of people seemed to blame the sheriff. Their attitude was that he should have solved the murder instantly instead of taking a couple of days. Then the team would have had time to settle down and get ready for the game.

Rhodes didn't want to talk about it. He said, "Where did he go when he left The County Line?"

Tuffy shrugged. "I figured he went home."

"Was he driving his car?"

Tuffy scratched at a scab under his right ear. He was wearing a greasy Dallas Cowboys cap, jeans, and a dirty shirt covered with a paisley pattern. His hair was cut so short on the sides that his scalp showed through, but he had sideburns that extended below his earlobes.

"I guess he was. He wouldn't have walked all the way out there."

"Did he ever run out of gas that you know of?"

"John? Hell, I never could get him to top off his tank. He'd run it down till it was nearly dry. I told him that the fuel pump'd pick up all kinds of trash off the bottom of the tank if he kept on like that, but he didn't listen. He said the gas gauge didn't work right anyway, but I knew that for a lie."

"Did he leave The County Line with anyone?"

"Not that I know of. Went off by himself, like always. He didn't have a woman or anything like that, if that's what you're thinking. He didn't run around on Kara. He just needed to get out of the house now and then. You a married man, Sheriff?"

Rhodes said that he was.

"Then you know what I mean. Man needs to get off to himself every now and then. I was married once myself, but it didn't take."

Rhodes didn't really know what Tuffy meant about the need to get off by himself. Rhodes had recently married for the second time, and he wasn't looking for ways to get away from Ivy. In fact, he wished he could find a way to spend more time in her company.

"I'd just as soon Kara didn't find out about where John and me was, though," Tuffy said. "It wouldn't do her any good to know he was out drinkin' when he could've been home with her."

Rhodes didn't make any promises.

"Do you have any idea why he might have been out there on that county road?" he asked.

"Not the least one. That's a long way from his

house, and he didn't know anybody out that way. Who was it found him?''

"David Grice."

"Yeah. I read his name in the paper. I never heard of him before, and I bet you John never did, either."

"What time did he leave The County Line?"

Tuffy scratched at the scab again. Rhodes was afraid it might come off. It didn't, but when he was finished with his scratching, Tuffy looked at his fingertips to make sure. There was grease under his nails, but no blood.

"I don't know about the time for sure," he said. "Maybe sometime around nine. Things were just getting going."

"And you don't have any idea who might have hit your brother and left the scene."

"If I did, I'd tell you. I want that son of a bitch caught and put behind bars, Sheriff. My brother and I were real close." Tuffy held up his crossed fingers. "Just like that. So you find that son of a bitch and put him where he belongs."

"I'll find him," Rhodes said, but so far he hadn't done it.

FIVE

"Do you think the two accidents are connected?" Ruth Grady asked.

Rhodes looked off into the trees to the south of the Burleson cabin. There was one that was filled with bright reddish orange fruit. Persimmons, Rhodes thought. He hadn't eaten a persimmon in years.

"I don't much like coincidences," he said. "Not that two accidents like these are necessarily a coincidence. People drown. People get killed by hit-and-run drivers."

"Not very often," Ruth said. "Not in Blacklin County, anyway."

She had a point. Rhodes couldn't remember the last hit-and-run he'd investigated before West's death, and the last drowning had been years before.

"But the accidents weren't anything alike," he said. "A hit-and-run and a drowning. They couldn't be more different."

"It still bothers me," Ruth said.

It bothered Rhodes, too.

RHODES DROVE BACK to the jail to do the paperwork on Pep Yeldell. When he got there, Hack and Lawton, the jailor, were waiting for him, Hack at his desk and Lawton leaning on a broom, both of them wearing expectant looks.

Rhodes figured that they wanted him to tell them about Yeldell's death, and he decided that he wouldn't. Whenever they knew something, he had to drag it out of them like a man pulling a stump out of swampy ground that just didn't want to let go. So he went to his desk, put on his reading glasses, and started to write.

"What you need," Hack said after a while, "is a computer in your car."

Rhodes didn't say anything. Hack, who was somewhere in his seventies, probably the latter part of them, was the one who had complained for a long time before Rhodes was finally able to persuade the county commissioners to get a computer for the department. But Hack still wasn't satisfied.

"If you had one in the car," Hack said, "you could enter your reports right there on the scene. Save 'em on a disk, and you'd have 'em ready to print out when you got back here to the office."

"Sounds like a good idea to me," Lawton said.

The jailer was as old as Hack, but Hack had seniority in the department and didn't like for Lawton to try to steer the conversations. Rhodes stayed quiet, waiting for Hack to ask about the body at the Old Settlers' Grounds.

But Hack didn't ask. He said, "I got a call while you were out there investigatin'."

Rhodes sighed, took off his glasses, folded them, and slipped them in his pocket. He should have known. There could have been only two reasons why Hack wouldn't have been asking about the body. One was that Hack already knew something, which was highly likely, especially if the ambulance crew had talked on the radio. And the other, even more likely, was that Hack knew something new, something that Rhodes didn't know.

"Who called?" Rhodes asked, hoping for a quick answer but knowing that it wasn't going to be that easy.

"Friend of yours," Lawton said.

Hack said, "I'm the one took the call."

"I know it," Lawton said. "I was just tryin' to be helpful."

Rhodes tried not to smile. The last thing that either of them wanted to be was helpful, at least not until they'd had their fun.

"A friend of mine?" he said.

"Preacher friend," Lawton said.

Hack twisted in his chair to glare at him. "You didn't take the call. I took it. I'm the one knows who called."

"I didn't say any different."

"Who called?" Rhodes asked, trying to stall the argument.

Hack turned back to him. "Brother Alton from the Free Will Church of the Lord Jesus is who called. You and him had a little round when you were foolin' with that emu rustlin' business."

"I know Brother Alton. What did he want?"

As soon as he'd said it, Rhodes knew he'd made a mistake. If he'd let Hack keep talking, the dispatcher might have let something slip. But now that

Rhodes had asked a direct question, Hack would take even longer to get to the point.

"You know how those preachers are," Hack said.

"Always messin' in other people's business," Lawton added.

Hack twisted in the chair again.

"You don't have to say it," Lawton told him. "I didn't take the call."

"Durn right, you didn't." Hack faced Rhodes. "He was calling about something that has to do with the Old Settlers' Grounds. I thought that was kinda interestin', considerin' where you were at the time."

Rhodes was interested too, but he didn't say anything. If he did, he might never find out what he wanted to know.

Hack looked over at his computer. "The ones that go in your car ain't all that big, you know. They're like the size of a notebook that you carry to school."

"I don't go to school," Lawton said.

"Yeah, and you prob'ly never did," Hack said. "You prob'ly stayed at home and—"

"We're getting off the subject," Rhodes said, taking a chance.

"I guess we are," Hack said. "It's Lawton's fault, though. He never—"

"Just tell me about the phone call," Rhodes said, his tone a little sharper than usual.

"All right, then," Hack said. "You don't have to get all huffed up about it. You and Ivy gettin' along all right? You seem mighty cranky today."

"Ivy and I are getting along fine. Tell me what Brother Alton wanted."

"Okay, but I hope you and Ivy ain't havin' any trouble. A man who don't keep regular hours and all can get out of touch at home if he's not careful."

"I appreciate your concern," Rhodes said. "Now, about that phone call."

"Yeah. Seems like Brother Alton's a little bit upset with the Sons and Daughters of Texas and their plans for the big celebration next summer."

"Why?" Rhodes asked.

"Well, he says the word on the street is that there's gonna be some un-Christian goin's-on there."

"'The word on the street'?"

"That's what they say on those cop shows on TV," Lawton said. "What it means is—"

"Never mind," Rhodes said. "I know what it means. What kind of un-Christian goings-on is Brother Alton worried about?"

"Indian dances," Hack said.

"Indian dances?"

"Native American dances," Lawton said. "See, Columbus thought he was goin' to India, and—"

"I guess you did go to school, after all," Hack said. "I guess you're gonna show off your education now and tell us all about how the Indians got their name, and—"

"Forget it," Rhodes said. "Just tell me about the dances."

Hack looked at Lawton. "See what I mean? Cranky."

Lawton nodded and opened his mouth to say something.

Rhodes gave him a warning look. "Don't say it. Just let Hack get back to the point."

Lawton closed his mouth and shook his head.

Hack said, "Downright cranky. Anyway, it seems like Ty Berry's been in touch with some tribe of Indians from over in East Texas. They're gonna come in and do some of their dances at the Old Settlers' Days. Brother Alton says that's paganism and a 'bomination in the sight of the Lord. Least that's what I think he said."

"And what does he expect me to do about it?" Rhodes asked.

"He didn't tell me that. But he said that you're the sheriff and that if you don't stop that dancin' at the Old Settlers' Grounds, there's gonna be trouble."

"There's already been trouble," Rhodes said. "There was a dead man out there this morning."

"Yeah," Hack said. "You think the preacher killed him?"

"It's a thought," Rhodes said.

SIX

LIKE THE Old Settlers' Grounds, the Free Will Church of the Lord Jesus was in better shape these days than it had been on Rhodes's last visit. The sign in front of the building had been repainted, as had the building itself. The windows all had glass in them, and the glass was clean. The roof had new shingles, and there was even a new doorknob on the door to the little room that jutted out to the side of the church and served as Brother Alton's office.

The inside of the office had also undergone some renovation and improvement. Someone had stripped the old dark varnish off Brother Alton's desk and put on a new coat of a lighter color. The windows had been washed and thin white curtains had been hung over them. Formerly, all the light in the room had come through the windows, but now there was an electric light fixture on the ceiling.

"Your church seems to be prospering," Rhodes said.

"The Lord has blessed us," Brother Alton said. "To a certain extent."

The preacher was lean and lanky and, unlike his church, hadn't changed a bit since his last encounter with Rhodes. He was wearing what appeared to be the very same black suit, the same wide black tie, and the same white shirt. He sat rigid and unsmiling behind his desk, and his rimless glasses reflected the light from the ceiling fixture.

"Fresh paint," Rhodes said. "Electricity in the office. A new roof. It all looks good."

"It is good," Brother Alton said. "Except for the roof."

"What's wrong with the roof?"

"It is a sham and a fraud. It mocks the Lord."

Rhodes wasn't sure how a roof could mock the Lord, but Brother Alton was glad to enlighten him.

"It leaks," the preacher said. "In ten places."

"That's not good," Rhodes agreed.

"It's a crime," Brother Alton said. "And I want the culprit arrested at once."

Rhodes was confused. "I thought you called about the Indian dancers."

Brother Alton sighed the sigh of a man who had to confront so much evil that it was hard to know where to begin describing it.

"I did call about that," he said. "But since that time I've had a conversation with Mr. Randall Overton. The dancers are an evil that is not yet present in our community, and we can stop them later. Right now we have to deal with the devil that lives among us. I have his address right here."

Brother Alton rummaged through the papers that covered his newly varnished desk and finally located a page that looked as if it had been torn from a legal pad. He pulled the page from under a large leather-covered Bible and handed it to Rhodes.

"I want to charge Mr. Overton with fraud," Brother Alton said.

Rhodes looked at the paper. "What fraud would that be?"

"He promised to fix our roof," Brother Alton said. "Fool that I am, I believed him. I even paid him in advance."

"Big mistake," Rhodes said.

"Amen," Brother Alton responded. "Oh, he did put shingles on the roof, but they don't do any good at all. In fact, they made things even worse than they were before he put them on. Now, if it so much as drizzles, water pours into the sanctuary. It can be very distracting to a congregation when water is streaming over them during the sermon."

"Might keep them awake," Rhodes said.

Brother Alton stared at him with no trace of a smile.

"Just a little joke," Rhodes said. "Not a very good one, I guess."

Another joke suddenly occurred to him, something about baptism, but he repressed it. He didn't think Brother Alton would appreciate that one, either.

Confirming Rhodes's suspicion, Brother Alton said, "The work of the Lord is nothing to joke about."

"I know," Rhodes said. "And I apologize. But I'm afraid you can't have Overton arrested for fraud."

"I have a contract," Brother Alton said. He opened a desk drawer and began to dig around in it. "It's right in here somewhere."

"It won't matter," Rhodes said. "Why did you

suddenly decide that having Overton arrested was so urgent?''

"Because of what he said when I spoke to him just now. He said that he'd done all he could, that he'd spent all the money we paid him on materials for the job, and that he wasn't going to do anything more, no matter how much the roof leaked. When I asked to see the receipts for materials, he actually laughed at me. Then he hung up."

"He's a crook, all right," Rhodes said. "Or a con man. But you can't get him for fraud. Now deceptive business practices, that's something else again. You might get him on that. It's not a felony, though."

"I want that man in jail and out of circulation. He's a menace to the community."

"I agree with you, but probably the best you can hope for is to get a judgment against him for the money."

"God will provide a judgment for him if the law of man can't."

"I wasn't talking about that kind of judgment," Rhodes said.

"I know. But the kind of judgment you're talking about is a joke. He'll never pay it. He'll laugh about it."

Brother Alton was probably right, Rhodes thought. It was too bad there was no good way to get a con man like Overton off the streets. Rhodes would have a little talk with him. He might not be able to arrest him, but he could discourage him from cheating anyone else.

"I'll see what I can do," he told Brother Alton. "But I came here to talk about something different."

"All right, we can talk about my call. I know you understand why I can't sit still and allow a pagan dance at a celebration of the people who settled this county. It's not right. It's an abomination before the Lord."

"The dance might not be one that's part of any religious ceremony," Rhodes said.

"It's still a pagan dance. I won't sit still for it."

"Do you ever go out to the Old Settlers' Grounds?" Rhodes asked.

Brother Alton didn't seem to understand the relevance of the question. "What?"

"Do you ever pay a visit to the Grounds, just to look around or see what's been done?"

Brother Alton turned to look out the window, apparently realized that the new curtains, though thin, obscured the view, and turned back to Rhodes.

"Why do you ask?"

"I was just curious."

"I may have been out there a time or two," Brother Alton said. "I'm interested in our county's history."

Rhodes wondered about that. There was always the chance that Brother Alton had been out at the Grounds for less honorable reasons.

"Did you ever climb a tree while you were there?" he asked.

Brother Alton looked even more confused than he

had earlier. "I'm not sure I follow you, Sheriff. Why would I want to climb a tree?"

To tie a rope in it, Rhodes thought, but he said, "Do you know a man named Pep Yeldell?"

Brother Alton gave it a moment's thought. "He's not a member of my congregation," he said, as if anyone else wasn't really worth knowing. "Why are you asking these questions? They don't have anything to do with my call."

"Yeldell drowned this morning, out at the Old Settlers' Grounds."

Brother Alton sat up straighter. "In one of the swimming pools?"

"Yes," Rhodes said. "How did you know that?"

"I didn't know. It was only a guess. Where else would he drown? The river? No one would swim in the river. Those pools are a menace. They should be drained and covered over."

"The river feeds them," Rhodes said. "There's not really any easy way to drain them. Ty Berry has already suggested it."

"There might be another tragedy, then," Brother Alton said. "I think the Grounds themselves should be closed to prevent the possibility."

"That would solve your problem with the dancers, wouldn't it?"

Brother Alton sat back. "I don't think I like the way you said that, Sheriff."

"I didn't mean anything by it," Rhodes said, but of course he had.

"The Lord works in mysterious ways," Brother

Alton said. "It may be that the death of this unfortunate man—what did you say his name was?"

"Pep Yeldell."

"It may be that the death of Pep Yeldell is the Lord's way of telling us that the Old Settlers' Grounds are unsafe and that there should be no celebrations there."

"It may be that Mr. Yeldell was drunk and didn't know what he was doing. There won't be any liquor served at the celebration."

"And thank the Lord for that," Brother Alton said. "But there will be liquor there, you can be sure of that. People will bring it in themselves if they can't buy it. There are always those who try to get around the law."

"My deputies and I will do our best to be sure no one gets around it during the celebration."

"And I'll do my best to help you," Brother Alton said.

Rhodes wondered just what he meant by that.

SEVEN

IT WAS NEARLY noon when Rhodes left Brother Alton's office, so he decided to go by the insurance office where Ivy worked and see if she wanted some lunch.

When he opened the door of the office, he thought about how different it looked from his own offices, the one at the jail and the one at the courthouse. The insurance office had pictures on the freshly painted walls, practically new carpet on the floor, and green plants that Rhodes couldn't begin to identify growing in pots on wrought-iron stands and in baskets that hung from the ceiling.

Ivy looked up and saw him.

"What a surprise," she said, and smiled. "A nice one, of course."

Rhodes liked her smile, her short, graying hair, and just about everything else about her.

"I thought you might like to go to lunch with me," he said.

Ivy closed the notebook she was writing in and stood up. "I sure would. When was the last time we had lunch together?"

Rhodes couldn't remember. For that matter, he couldn't remember the last time he'd had lunch, period. In his job, he didn't always get to stop work just because the noon hour had arrived.

Before he'd married Ivy, he had sometimes managed to slip home for a bologna sandwich, but Ivy had convinced him that bologna and Miracle Whip on white bread wasn't exactly the best combination for someone who was worried about his waistline, which Rhodes was. When he had time to think about it, that is.

"It's not approved by the American Heart Association, either," she had told him.

So Rhodes had begun to try to eat a slightly more healthy diet, and while he still didn't eat a regular lunch, he at least ate one lower in fat and calories. Most of the time. There was only so much a man could stand.

He also tried to spend a little time every day on his stationary bike, but he didn't always have time for that, any more than he had time for lunch.

Still, over the course of the last few months he'd lost a few pounds, and he was almost able to see his belt buckle when he looked straight down. Not quite, but it was a small belt buckle, not one of those giant models like the one on Pep Yeldell's belt. Anyway, he was working on it. Give him another month or two, and he'd be able to see it, all right.

"Where would you like to eat?" Ivy asked, picking up her purse from the floor by her chair.

Rhodes thought about it. He'd had cereal and fruit with skim milk for breakfast, and for supper the previous evening Ivy had made vegetable sandwiches with broccoli, melted low-fat mozzarella cheese, sun-dried tomatoes, mushrooms, and red and green bell peppers.

He'd had about all the healthy diet he could stand for a while.

"How about a bacon cheeseburger?" he said. "They're on special at the Dairy Queen."

"On special?" Ivy said.

"A dollar ninety-nine. Not including fries. We wouldn't have to get fries."

"What about a Heath Bar Blizzard?"

"I guess we could have one of those," Rhodes said. "But only if you insist."

Ivy grinned. "I insist," she said.

THE DAIRY QUEEN WAS crowded at noon, but Rhodes didn't mind. He was just glad it wasn't Bean Day. Beans and cornbread were fine, and they were also low in fat. But today his mouth was set for a bacon cheeseburger.

He parked near the red-and-white sign, and they went inside. Rhodes took a deep breath, inhaling the reassuring odors of bacon and burgers frying on the grill, chicken strips and potatoes frying in deep vats of grease. He could practically feel the plaque accumulating on the walls of his arteries. He also thought he could feel the waistband of his pants tighten around his own waist, but he didn't care. It was a bacon cheeseburger or nothing.

Ivy found a booth while Rhodes ordered. He paid for the food and took the numbered slip that the young woman behind the counter handed him.

"Two-seventeen," he said, sliding onto the bench across the table from Ivy, who was looking over the crowd.

"Do you know anyone in this place?" she asked.
Rhodes looked around.

"I recognize a face or two. But I don't really
know any of them."

"Me neither," Ivy said. "And I grew up here.
Where do all these people come from?"

Rhodes didn't know. It was a question that had
often puzzled him. There was no industry in Clearview, and there wasn't much farming. The cotton
gin had closed more than thirty years ago.

"Some of them work at the power plant, I
guess," he said, referring to the large coal-burning
facility on one end of the county. "And some of
them have always lived here without us knowing
them. Some of them work in Dallas or Waco and
commute. It's not that bad a drive. Some of them
ranch, maybe, or have small farms. A lot of them
are probably retired. It's just that we don't get out
much. No wonder we don't know anyone."

"They know who you are, though," Ivy said.

Rhodes supposed that was true. He didn't wear a
uniform or dress in any way that would call attention
to himself. He didn't even wear a ten-gallon hat like
a lot of sheriffs did, but people knew who he was.

"It goes with the job," he said.

"Speaking of the job, what's been happening?"

Rhodes told her about Pep Yeldell.

"Another fatal accident? That makes two."

"You're thinking that it's too much of a coincidence, aren't you?" Rhodes said.

"Maybe it comes from living with a lawman.

Have you found out whether there's any connection between Yeldell and the other one? John West?''

"Not yet. I'm going over to Ballinger's and talk to Dr. White later. Maybe he'll tell me that it was just an accident, that Yeldell had been drinking and just fell in the pool.''

"Does that mean you think Yeldell was drunk?''

"Not necessarily. He got drunk often enough. But we won't know about this time until later. We'll have to send blood samples off to the pathology lab, and we'll be lucky to get results in a week.''

"So how will you know if it was an accident?''

Rhodes started to tell her, but the woman from behind the counter came to their booth. She was carrying a red tray that held two cardboard baskets and two tall paper cups.

"Number two-seventeen?'' she said.

"That's us,'' Rhodes said, sliding his receipt across the table.

The woman put the tray on the table. Each basket held a bacon cheeseburger wrapped in white paper. There were two small paper containers of salt and one of pepper beside the burgers, along with two paper-wrapped plastic straws.

"Get you anything else?'' the woman asked.

"No thanks,'' Rhodes told her.

"No fries? Onion rings?''

"Not today,'' Ivy said.

The woman shrugged. "Enjoy your meal.''

Rhodes pulled the paper off his straw and stuck it through the plastic lid on the cup. Then he took a drink. Dr Pepper from a fountain was never as good as when it came from a bottle or can. It always seemed to lack an essential ingredient—syrup or fizz or something.

The bacon cheeseburger was much more satisfying.

Ivy let him eat about half of it before she asked again, "So how will you know if it was an accident?"

"It depends on what Dr. White finds. If Yeldell didn't have water in his lungs, that means he didn't drown. He was killed some other way and dumped in the pool."

Ivy wiped mustard from the corner of her mouth with a paper napkin. "What if he did drown?"

"Then it was probably an accident. Just a case of a bad combination of a rotten tree limb and a man who'd had too much to drink."

"Who put that rope there, anyway?" Ivy asked.

"That's a good question. Ty Berry thinks Faye Knape did it, in hopes that something like the Yeldell thing would happen. That way the Sons and Daughters of Texas would be discredited, and it would be easier to get the Burleson cabin moved to the courthouse lawn."

"Do the commissioners want it there?"

"I don't think so. No one's said so, anyway."

"Then I don't see why Faye would put a rope in a tree. I'll bet someone just put it there for fun and didn't take it down."

That was what Rhodes thought, too, but he said, "There's someone else who wouldn't mind seeing the Sons and Daughters discredited and putting a stop to that celebration they have planned for the summer.''

"Who's that?''

Rhodes told her about Brother Alton.

"He's certainly become righteous since that emu business,'' Ivy said. "Did you remind him of that?''

"No. Righteous seems to agree with him. The church is taking in quite a bit of money. They've got a new roof, new paint, clean windows.''

He didn't mention the problems with the roof.

"I think putting a rope in a tree would be a pretty silly way to try to stop a celebration,'' Ivy said.

"Me too,'' Rhodes said. "There's another thing that bothers me about that rope, too.''

"What's that?''

"Why would anyone tie a rope around a rotten limb?''

"I don't know. Do you?''

"Maybe,'' Rhodes said.

EIGHT

THE HEATH BAR BLIZZARD was even more satisfying than the bacon cheeseburger, and Rhodes felt excessively virtuous because he ordered only a small one. He finished it quickly and waited for Ivy to finish hers.

"I don't see how you can eat ice cream so fast," she said, taking a small bite from the red plastic spoon.

"It's easy. I don't bother to chew it. I just swallow it straight down."

"That's not true, and you know it. A sheriff shouldn't lie to one of his constituents."

"Are you sure you voted for me?"

"I will next time. I promise."

When Ivy had finished her Blizzard, Rhodes put everything on the plastic tray and took it to the wastebasket. He dumped the trash in the wastebasket and put the plastic tray on top.

"What now?" Ivy asked.

"Time to go back to work," he said.

RUTH GRADY was waiting at the jail when Rhodes got there. Pep Yeldell's parents had died years before in a car wreck in West Texas, but the county was full of Yeldell's aunts, uncles, and cousins. Ruth had been talking to some of them.

"They don't know much about him," she said. "He wasn't big on family. He worked at Lowery's Paint and Body, he liked to go out and have a good time, and they're sorry he's dead. That's about all they could tell me."

"Can't hold likin' to have a good time against a man," Hack said from his desk, where he was watching a soap opera on his tiny TV set. "A work-in' man needs to get out for a little fun now and then."

"How's Miz McGee getting along?" Ruth asked.

Miz McGee was the woman that Hack had been squiring around for the last few months. He didn't like to talk about her in the office when Lawton was around because Lawton was likely to make light-minded remarks. But the jailor was upstairs cleaning a cell, and Hack didn't mind talking.

"She's just fine," Hack said. "We might rent us a video tonight if we can find a good one."

"What's good these days?" Ruth asked.

"I'd like to see that one with the stealth bomber in it," Hack said. "*Broken Arrow,* it's called. I've liked that John Travolta ever since he played in that movie they filmed down in Houston."

"Urban Cowboy?"

"That's the one. They filmed that at Mickey Gilley's nightclub. You ever been there?"

"No," Ruth said. "Have you?"

"Yeah. I was down in Pasadena to visit a cousin of mine one time, and we went out there."

Throughout this conversation, Rhodes sat at his desk wondering if Ruth, in only a few short months, had become as adept as Hack and Lawton at avoiding the topic at hand.

But Ruth had only been making conversation and cultivating Hack. She turned her attention to Rhodes and got back to the subject.

"That liking a good time I mentioned? The thing about Yeldell is that he liked women quite a bit. Maybe even more than Hack does."

Hack laughed. "I doubt that," he said, and turned back to his soap opera.

"Yeldell didn't draw the line at married women, either," Ruth said. "According to one of his cousins, there're quite a few married men who won't be too upset to hear the news of the drowning."

"What cousin would that be?" Rhodes asked.

"Gary Heckethorn. He works at the MiniMarket out on the Thurston highway."

"Did he give you any names?"

Ruth handed Rhodes a piece of paper torn from a small spiral notebook. "I wrote them down."

Rhodes glanced at the paper. He didn't recognize any of the names. He folded the paper and stuck it in his shirt pocket.

"Did Heckethorn say whether Yeldell knew John West?" he asked.

"He said West's name was familiar, but that's all. He said maybe West was somebody Yeldell met out at The County Line. Heckethorn went there with Yeldell some, and he says they might have met West there. But he's not sure. They met a lot of people at The County Line."

"We might have to talk to Heckethorn again," Rhodes said. "And Tuffy West."

"I wish we could find John West's car," Ruth said. "That still worries me."

It worried Rhodes, too. There was no reason for the car not to have turned up by now. He had put out an APB on it, but it hadn't been reported.

"That car could be in Russia by now," Hack said. He turned off his TV set, no longer interested in the soap opera. "I read an article in the paper just the other day about how all the big-time Russian criminals have come over here to the U.S.A. now that the Soviet Union's collapsed. They're gonna be bigger than the Mafia, is what the article said. One thing they're doin' is stealin' cars and sendin' 'em clear back over there to Russia. What kinda car did West have?"

"It wasn't a car, exactly," Rhodes said. "It was a Jeep Cherokee."

"There you go, then," Hack said. "That's the very model those Russians like the best of all. It's prob'ly mushin' through the snow drifts up there in Siberia right now."

Somehow Rhodes found it hard to believe that a car stolen in Blacklin County, Texas, could have found its way to Russia. Mexico, maybe, but not Russia.

"If it sat out on one of those county roads very long," Hack said, "it was fair game for anybody that came along and wanted it. It'd be just like some Russian gang to take it. I haven't trusted Russians since they pulled the wool over F.D.R.'s eyes at Yalta after World War Two.''

"I looked for the car that night," Rhodes said. "It wasn't anywhere around.''

"Must not've looked very good," Hack said.

"I looked good. And Ruth looked with me the next day.''

"Too late by then. Russians already had it.''

"I thought the Russians were pretty much confined to the eastern part of the country," Ruth said.

Hack gave her a pitying look. "That's what they'd *like* you to believe.''

"Let's assume just for a minute that the Russians don't have the Cherokee," Rhodes said. "What else could have happened to it?''

"*Somebody's* got it," Hack said. "You can laugh about the Russians if you want to, but somebody's got that car. It's too nice a ride to be sittin' in some bar ditch somewhere.''

That was a point Rhodes could agree with.

"Maybe we've just been looking in the wrong places," Ruth said.

That was another point Rhodes could agree with. He just didn't know where else to look.

Ruth didn't either, but she had another idea.

"What if he was with someone that night? Have we considered that possibility?''

"No," Rhodes said. "But if he was with someone, why was he carrying a gas can?''

"It didn't have to be *his* car that ran out of gas," Ruth said.

NINE

"I ALREADY TOLD YOU," Tuffy West said. "I was with John at The County Line that night. We had a couple of beers, maybe three, and that was it. John left. I thought he was headed home."

"And you didn't see Pep Yeldell that night?"

"Don't remember," Tuffy said.

They were inside the multipurpose building that sat near the front of Tuffy's wrecking yard. It smelled of oil and the old tires that were stacked high along one wall. Tuffy was behind a high wooden counter that looked as if it had been built about the time F.D.R. was getting fooled by Hack's Russians at Yalta. Behind him, wooden shelves reached all the way to the ceiling. They were crammed with all sorts of used auto parts: generators, distributors, carburetors, thermostats, radios, tape players, and hundreds of other grease-and-oil-covered items that Rhodes couldn't identify. There was a wooden stepladder leaning against the shelves.

There was a Pontiac Firebird sitting nearby on the concrete floor. The fenders were accordioned, and the front bumper was pushed up almost to the passenger compartment. Rhodes hadn't worked the wreck, but Ruth had told him about it. Drinking and driving don't mix.

On past the Firebird there was another car with

its hood raised high, its engine held above the empty engine compartment on a chain hoist.

"But you did know Yeldell?" Rhodes said.

Tuffy shrugged. "Everybody knew Pep. He was around out there a lot of the time."

"Who was he with?"

"Different people."

"Women?" Rhodes asked.

"Most of the time. He was a pretty good-lookin' guy, you know? And there are a lot of ladies out there tryin' to find somebody to have fun with."

"He won't be out there anymore," Rhodes said.

Tuffy said, "Why not?"

"He drowned last night. Out at the Old Settlers' Grounds."

"What the hell was he doin' out there?"

"Swimming. At least that's what it looks like he was doing."

Tuffy moved a scratch pad out of his way and leaned his forearms on the counter.

"That's a damn shame. Pep was a good ol' boy. Knew how to have a good time," he said. He looked over at the Firebird, then back at Rhodes. "Was he by himself out there?"

"Looks that way," Rhodes said.

"You wouldn't think old Pep'd go out there for a swim by himself. You sure there wasn't some woman with him?"

"I'm not sure of anything at this point," Rhodes said. "I'm just trying to find out what I can."

That was basically the way Rhodes got things done. Hack could talk all he wanted to about modern crime detection methods and computers, but Rhodes still believed that talking, listening, and thinking were more likely to get him to a solution than all the computers in the world. He knew he might be fooling himself, but usually he got results.

He hadn't gotten very far with locating John West's killer, however, as Tuffy reminded him.

"I don't see how this is helpin' you find out who ran over John," Tuffy said.

"If he and Yeldell knew each other, there might be some connection between their deaths," Rhodes said.

"Hell, they knew each other. I told you that. I said that everybody knew Pep, and everybody included John. They weren't what you'd call best friends, but they'd drink a beer now and then."

"But not the night John got killed."

"Not that I remember. But they could've met somewhere else that night. If John got killed when you say he did, he didn't go home. He might've gone to some other club, had some more to drink. Maybe Pep was there. Why, you think somebody killed Pep?"

"It could have been an accident," Rhodes said.

"I expect so. Pep wasn't what you'd call a careful man. I've seen him get in fights, take on two or three guys at a time if he had a drink or two in him."

Rhodes didn't often get called out to The County Line when there was a fight. The management liked to settle things without resorting to calling the law. But he'd been there a time or two, when things got out of hand. He didn't recall that Pep had been involved, however.

"Did Pep fool around with other men's wives?" Rhodes asked.

Tuffy straightened and crossed his arms over his chest. "I wouldn't know about that. You don't see a whole lot of weddin' rings out at The County Line."

"What about Gary Heckethorn? You know him?"

"Seen him couple of times. I know him to talk to. Why?"

"He's Yeldell's cousin. He was with him at The County Line now and then."

"You're tryin' too hard, Sheriff," Tuffy said. "I don't think John knew Heckethorn any better'n I did, and we didn't know Pep Yeldell very well, either. I don't think John's killin' has anything to do with Yeldell."

Rhodes was pretty sure he agreed with West, but he still didn't like the idea of two accidental deaths so close together, and he didn't like the fact that he was no closer to finding West's killer than he'd been when the accident happened.

"You let me know when you find out somethin' you can get your teeth into, hear?" Tuffy said.

Rhodes promised that he would.

CLYDE BALLINGER'S funeral home had once been one of Clearview's finest homes, a family mansion with a swimming pool, tennis courts, and landscaped grounds that covered an entire block. But times had changed. The last member of the family that owned the house and property had died, and Clyde had bought the old estate for his business. He had his office in back of the funeral home, in a little brick building that had been the servants' quarters.

Rhodes didn't know about the rest of the building, but the room where Clyde had his office was cluttered with the old paperback books that Clyde bought at garage sales. They generally didn't cost him more than a quarter, and he argued that they gave him a lot more entertainment than some fat new novel that he'd have to pay six-ninety-nine for.

He was sitting at his desk reading something called *China Coast* by Don Smith when Rhodes came in.

"Is that a good one?" Rhodes asked.

"Darn right," Ballinger said, putting a thin slip of paper in the book to mark his place. He closed the book and looked at the back cover. "It says here, 'a real nose-busting adventure.' Now is that the kind of thing that makes you want to read a book or not?"

"I'm not sure," Rhodes said.

"Well, it makes me want to read it." Ballinger put down *China Coast* and picked up another book that lay on his desk. "I found this one today, too."

He held it up so Rhodes could see the cover. *A Fiend in Need* by someone named Milton K. Ozaki.

"They don't write 'em like this anymore," Ballinger said, giving the book a little shake for emphasis.

"I'll bet they don't," Rhodes said.

Ballinger put the book down. "You probably didn't come by to talk about great literature, though, did you?"

"Not today," Rhodes said.

Ballinger looked at the ceiling. "Or football?"

"Especially not football."

"Guess you must want to talk about Dr. White's report on Pep Yeldell, then."

"You guess right."

Ballinger opened a desk drawer and took out a small stack of papers.

"Got it right here. He finished a little while ago."

He handed the papers to Rhodes, who started reading. Ballinger watched for a second, then picked up *China Coast* and opened it to his place.

After a while, Rhodes said, "So Yeldell drowned."

Ballinger marked his spot in the book again. "That's what Dr. White said. Water in his lungs."

"What about the bump on his head?"

"Looks like he was hit by a tree limb. The limb knocked him out, and he drowned. It's all in there about the little pieces of tree bark in the scalp."

"I saw it. Dr. White saved the bark, I'm sure."

"He's got it all bagged and tagged. Took blood samples, too. Those are ready to go to the lab."

"I've got a tree limb in the evidence locker at the jail that I want to try to match up to the bark from Yeldell's scalp," Rhodes said. "Anything I missed in this?"

"Nope. Dr. White says Yeldell was most likely

drunk and drowned when he got hit by that limb. You know who hit him with it?''

"It fell out of a tree,'' Rhodes said.

"Oh. Well, in that case, what you've got is an accident.'' Ballinger thought about that for a second. "Seems like we're having a lot of those around here lately.''

"Accidents happen,'' Rhodes said.

"You have to wonder about that hit-and-run, though.''

"Why?''

"Well, it looks like if it was an accident, whoever did it would come forward, tell the truth, and get it over with.''

"Not if whoever did it was drunk or driving recklessly at the time.''

"You find any sign of that at the scene?''

"No,'' Rhodes said. "But that road's not the kind that takes tracks.''

"You never know about accidents like that, I guess,'' Ballinger said.

"Eventually you do,'' Rhodes told him. "If you keep after it.''

"And you're going to keep after it, am I right?'' He picked up *China Coast*. "That's what the tough guys always do.''

"I'm not a tough guy,'' Rhodes said. "But I'm not going to quit.''

Ballinger smiled. "I didn't think you would.''

TEN

WHEN RHODES WANTED to think things over, he usually went to his office in the county courthouse, a building that he thought vaguely resembled the Kremlin but that the few tourists that came to Blacklin County seemed to think was well worth photographing. The building was old, Rhodes had to admit that, but he didn't see the beauty of it.

What he liked about it was the fact that it was quiet, especially on the floor where his office was located, away from the courtrooms and the noise of the really busy offices, like that of the tax assessor-collector, which was down in the basement. He liked the wide marble halls and the high ceilings, too. There had been some talk about modernizing the building, lowering the ceilings and blocking the windows to reduce the cost of heating and cooling, but so far nothing had come of it. Rhodes hoped that nothing would. He figured it was worth a few dollars to preserve a little of the dignity of the past.

Another thing Rhodes liked about the courthouse was the Dr Pepper machine, where he could actually get a Dr Pepper in a glass bottle. Of course he'd already had one Dr Pepper that day, but it hadn't been a very good one, so he figured it didn't count. He'd skip the cheese crackers with peanut butter this time, though.

He put his two quarters in the old green Dr Pepper machine, pushed the button, and took the glass bottle when it slid out. He opened it and went to his office to drink it.

He closed the door behind him, sat in the swivel chair, and put his feet up on his desk.

What he had was two accidents with not very much connecting them other than the fact that the two dead men might have known one another slightly. That wasn't exactly strange in Blacklin County. Though Rhodes and Ivy hadn't known anyone in the Dairy Queen, it wasn't unusual at all for either of them to run into quite a few people they knew nearly any day of the week. Blacklin County didn't have the population of metropolitan Houston, after all.

So why did Rhodes think the two accidents might be connected? There was no real reason at all. It was just a feeling he had, a hunch. It was almost like a physical itch that he could feel right between his shoulder blades in that place that was just out of reach when you tried to scratch it.

Hack would tell him that a hunch didn't mean a thing and that the modern lawman should rely on the kind of information he could call up from his computer or get analyzed in the crime lab. But Rhodes had played hunches before and gotten good results. There were some things you couldn't analyze in a lab.

Rhodes drank the Dr Pepper and thought about West and Yeldell. West sold auto parts, and Yeldell worked in a body shop. Another tenuous connection, hardly worth thinking about, and it probably didn't mean a thing.

But it did, somehow. Rhodes wasn't sure how, but he could feel that itch again. It had to mean something. All he had to do was find out what.

He got up and left his office, putting the empty Dr Pepper bottle in the rack by the side of the machine as he passed by.

MRS. JOHN WEST, whose first name was Kara, lived in a modest house in one of the newer areas of Clearview, a section of the town that had been developed about twenty years previously when it appeared that there might be some renewed interest in drilling for oil and gas in the area.

In the early part of the century, Clearview had gone through an oil boom that the older members of the community still remembered with both fondness and regret, and the tall drilling rigs that remained behind had been a constant reminder of the boom to everyone else until fairly recently. The wells had been drilled so quickly that no one bothered to take down the rigs, which had rusted in the old fields until someone finally got the idea of selling them for scrap.

The new boom hadn't happened, of course. A few gas wells were successfully drilled, but there wasn't much oil, and gas wasn't selling for anything that would make a man rich, not unless he was lucky enough to get several wells in the same unit. Rhodes didn't know of anyone who'd been that lucky.

The houses that had been built in anticipation of

the town's growth had been kept up pretty well by the people who bought them, though a few of them were obviously abandoned, probably owned now by mortgage holders in some place like California. Yellowing newspapers lay in yards that hadn't been mowed very often the previous summer and were now covered in tall dead or dying grass.

Kara West lived in a house that had once been in pretty bad shape, but her husband had fixed it up after they bought it, and it had gotten even nicer since his death. He might have been playing around on her, but he had believed in heavy life insurance, a quarter of a million dollars' worth.

When Mrs. West answered the door, she looked much happier than she had when Rhodes had last seen her several days after the funeral. She had been wearing an old black dress then, still in mourning, and she had been crying quite a bit.

Now she was wearing a new dress, her hair was stylishly cut and several shades blonder, and she obviously hadn't cried for quite a while. Thinking of the funeral and of the change in Mrs. West reminded Rhodes of something else.

"You go to Brother Alton's church, don't you?" he said.

"Yes," Mrs. West said. "Is that what you came here to ask me?"

"No, but I was thinking today that someone had made some generous donations to Brother Alton. That was a nice thing to do."

"I'm not saying I gave any money to the church. That's between me and the Lord and the I.R.S."

"I know," Rhodes said. "Could I come in for a minute?"

Mrs. West opened the door and Rhodes stepped through onto a newly tiled floor. Then he followed Mrs. West into a room with new carpet, a new couch, and two new wing chairs. There was a huge projection TV set on one wall.

"You've done some remodeling," Rhodes said.

"I had a little money for the first time in my life," Mrs. West said, "and I'd lost my husband. So I decided to change things around a little."

Rhodes didn't blame her, but for the first time he wondered about all that insurance money. He supposed he should have been suspicious right from the first, but Mrs. West's grief had seemed genuine at the time. She had spent the whole funeral crying on Tuffy's shoulder.

Mrs. West asked Rhodes to have a seat, so he took one of the wing chairs. It was more comfortable than it looked. Mrs. West sat on the couch, behind a new coffee table.

"Have you found something new about John?" she asked.

"Not exactly," Rhodes said. "But there's been another accidental death."

"A hit-and-run?"

"No. A drowning. A man named Pep Yeldell. Did you know him?"

"No," Mrs. West said, with no hesitation. "I never heard of him."

Rhodes wondered why she didn't at least have to

think about it for a second. So he said, "Your husband knew him, I think."

"I've found out a few things about John, myself," Mrs. West said. "He knew a lot of people that I didn't know. Most of them were women."

So liking women was something else that West and Yeldell had in common. Rhodes wondered if it meant anything. Rhodes also wondered who Mrs. West had been talking to. So he asked her.

She evaded the question. "No one in particular. Some of the people at the church have been kind enough to tell me a few things. I wonder why you didn't tell me, Sheriff."

Rhodes hadn't said anything to her because Tuffy West had told him that John didn't run around on his wife, a case of a brother not wanting to sully the reputation of the deceased, Rhodes supposed. Or maybe Mrs. West had been misinformed.

But he didn't say that, either. He said, "I didn't have any evidence of it."

"But you knew it?"

"No. And I still don't know that it's true."

"Oh, it was true, all right," Mrs. West said. "I'm certain of that. I was a fool for a long time, but I'm not quite so foolish now."

Rhodes looked around the room. "Your husband must have loved you. He left you well provided for."

"Guilt," Mrs. West said. "That's all it was. Love didn't have a thing to do with it."

Rhodes figured that if she were going to be bitter, he might as well take advantage of it. "Did anyone give you specific names?"

Mrs. West's blond hair shimmered when she shook her head. "No. But I don't need the names. I don't think I even want to know them."

"They might help me find out something about the accident."

"I don't think so. John was just in the wrong place at the wrong time. It seems like he was in the wrong place a lot of the time, come to think of it. Have you heard anything at all about the Cherokee?"

"Not a thing," Rhodes said. "But I'm still looking."

"I don't see how something that big can just disappear."

Rhodes didn't see how it could either, not unless Hack was right and the Russian Mafia, or whatever it was called, had hijacked it to the former Soviet Union. But he didn't see any need to mention that to Mrs. West.

So he said simply, "It might have been stolen."

"But wouldn't someone have found it by now?"

"Not necessarily. Just change the license plates, and it could be awfully hard to locate."

"I hope you can find it," Mrs. West said. "I really liked that car."

"I'll find it," Rhodes said with more confidence that he actually felt.

Mrs. West smiled, and Rhodes was surprised to see that she was wearing braces. He knew that more and more adults were wearing them, but it wasn't a common sight in Clearview.

"Call me when you do," she said.

ELEVEN

RANDALL OVERTON didn't live in a house nearly as well kept as Kara West's, and his neighborhood wasn't nearly as respectable, though long ago it had been.

Overton's house was on a street of similar wood-frame houses, all of which had been built along about the time of the oil boom and none of which had been cared for particularly well in the years since. Most of them needed paint, most of them had much more dirt in their yards than grass, and most showed signs of general neglect: an old tire in the front yard, a car up on blocks in the oil-stained driveway, a wringer-equipped washing machine sitting on the sagging front porch, chickens scratching in the dirt behind a picket fence that was missing several pickets.

Rhodes parked the county car in front of Overton's house. It was the one with the car up on blocks in the driveway. Rhodes couldn't tell what kind of car it was because it was covered by a cream-colored tarp.

Whatever it was, it wasn't Overton's only vehicle. There was a shiny new Toyota truck parked behind it. The roofing business evidently paid pretty well. At least the kind of roofing business that Overton conducted.

Rhodes was curious about the tarp-covered car. It didn't look as if it could be a Jeep Cherokee, but you never knew unless you looked. He'd heard of a hit-and-run case in Houston in which the car had sat in an apartment parking lot for two years before somebody looked at it.

So when he walked past the covered car, he lifted the tarp at the front for a look at the grille. He saw a vertical chrome fish mouth, which could mean only one thing: he was looking at a 1958 Edsel. His curiosity got the better of him, and he lifted the side of the tarp. The Edsel was a four-door hardtop, red and white, one of the ugliest cars ever made in the eyes of some beholders.

But not in the eyes of Rhodes. He was instantly in love. In Texas in 1958, fourteen-year-olds could get a learner's permit, but Rhodes hadn't been quite old enough even for that when Edsels appeared on the scene. Not that it mattered; to him they represented the high point of a decade in which Detroit seemed determined to make the gaudiest cars possible. He wondered whether Overton would sell the car or whether he was saving it for himself.

Rhodes lowered the tarp and walked to Overton's covered porch, which wasn't connected to the ground by any steps that Rhodes could see. He put one foot on the porch, grabbed one of the roof supports—a two-by-four nailed to the floor of the porch and one of the roof beams—and pulled himself up. He could hear muffled voices inside the house, but as he knocked on the rusty screen door he realized that the voices were coming from a TV set. Either that, or Overton had invited Oprah to come over for a visit and she had accepted.

No one answered his knock. He knocked harder, but there was still no response.

Rhodes stepped off the porch, which proved to be no easier than stepping up on it had been. About the time the Edsel had been new, he would have jumped both up and down with no trouble at all, but those days were long gone.

He walked around to the back of the house. There were three bundles of shingles and a stack of warped two-by-fours in the weeds near the steps leading to the back door. Rhodes was glad to see the steps. He mounted them and knocked on the door. There was no screen this time.

And there was no answer to the knock. Maybe Overton was out somewhere chiseling someone out of money for a worthless roofing job. Or maybe he was just asleep. Or the TV was too loud. Rhodes really did want to ask him about the Edsel. He hammered so hard on the door that it rattled loosely in the frame.

A dog started barking somewhere inside, and a man's voice yelled, "Shut up, you mutt!"

So Overton, or someone, was there after all. Rhodes knocked again. The dog continued to bark, but no one tried to quiet it again.

"All right, all right," the man's voice called. "Keep your britches on. I'm coming."

The back door opened and the barking got louder, though Rhodes couldn't see the dog.

He could, however, see a man who was bigger

than Rhodes had expected. He must have weighed two hundred pounds, and he was solid and wide.

The roofer was wearing a threadbare Joe Camel T-shirt that didn't quite reach the top of his faded jeans. He wasn't wearing a belt. No shoes, either. His head was completely bald, but there was hair coming out of every opening in the T-shirt, pushing up Overton's neck and down his arms. It made a furry fringe between the T-shirt and the jeans. It was as if a cheap sofa had exploded inside the T-shirt.

Overton looked at Rhodes without expression. It was possible that his face wasn't capable of much expression. It was almost flat, like the face of a cartoon character who's been hit by an iron. Even the nose was flat.

"Randall Overton?" Rhodes said.

"Yeah," Overton said. His voice was even flatter than his face. "So?"

Rhodes hated to have to show Overton his badge. It would probably mean the car deal was off. But there was nothing else to do.

"Sheriff Dan Rhodes," he said, producing the badge. "I'd like to talk to you for a minute."

Overton didn't appear to be unduly impressed by the badge or Rhodes's name.

"Talk about what?" he said.

"A roofing job."

"You got a bad roof you need fixed? A leak?"

"Not exactly."

"Well why do you want to talk about a roofing job, then?"

The dog was still barking, but it was quieter now. Rhodes could hear the TV again.

"Can I come inside?" he asked.

Overton didn't move. He just shifted his weight so that his feet were planted a little more firmly on the floor.

"We can talk just fine right here," he said.

Rhodes didn't push it. "All right. It's about the roofing job you did at the Free Will Church."

"What about it?" Overton sounded bored.

"It's a pretty sorry job. The roof still leaks, and Brother Alton tells me that you won't do anything about it."

Overton leaned against the door frame. "Can't. They won't pay me."

"They've already paid you."

"I did what I was paid for, and then some. I spent most of the money on materials. Didn't get hardly a thing for all my labor."

"Brother Alton says you won't show him the receipts for the materials."

Overton shrugged. "Lost 'em. He'll have to take my word for it. He's a Christian man, right? Why would I lie to him?"

"Because you're a con man and a swindler," Rhodes said.

Overton straightened up and looked at Rhodes with surprise.

"What are you sayin'?"

"Which word didn't you understand?"

Overton took a quick step forward, thrusting his chest out without bringing up his hands. He bumped into Rhodes, who almost lost his balance on the top step.

But not quite. He wasn't as agile as he had been when he was a kid, but he was still steady enough when he had to be.

When Overton tried to bump him again, Rhodes grabbed the front of Overton's T-shirt with one hand and the door frame with the other. Using Overton's momentum, Rhodes helped the roofer keep right on moving, past the steps and into the backyard.

Overton hit the ground with his legs churning, but he lost his equilibrium and stumbled to his knees. Before he could get to his feet, Rhodes was standing over him with his hand pushing down on his back.

"Think about it before you try anything," Rhodes said. "You wouldn't want to get arrested for assaulting a peace officer."

"You're the one that assaulted *me*," Overton said, but he didn't try to get up.

"We could let a judge decide that," Rhodes said, keeping his hand pressed against the small of Overton's back. He could feel the thick hair through the T-shirt. "If you really want to, that is."

"You called me a name," Overton said.

Rhodes nodded, though he was aware that Overton couldn't see it. He was a little surprised that Overton was so sensitive.

"That's right. I called you a con man. And a swindler, too, I think. I could have said you were a crook and a cheat and a few other things, but I didn't."

"I didn't cheat nobody."

"Sure you did. You cheated Brother Alton and his church. For all I know you've cheated other people around here, too, but they haven't told me about it yet. I'm going to ask around and find out. If you have, I'm going to see if I can get some of them to press charges."

"For what? Ever' time I hire on to do a job for people, I do it."

"But do you do it well? Or do you take the money, do a halfway job, and then claim you spent all the money on materials before you run out on the people who paid you?"

"I do the job right, dammit."

"I hope so," Rhodes said. "I don't want to have to arrest you for deceptive business practices."

"You won't be arrestin' me. I didn't deceive nobody."

"We'll see about that. I want you to finish the job on Brother Alton's roof, too. And I want you to do it right."

"I'll have to have a little something for my labor if I do."

"No you won't," Rhodes said. "You've already taken all the money you're going to take. Unless you can find those receipts and show them to me."

"You know I can't do that."

"Then you'll just have to finish the job for free. Either that or be arrested. Which do you want to do?"

"I'll finish the damn job."

"Good." Rhodes moved his hand off Overton's back and moved away. "You can stand up now."

Overton stood up and glowered at Rhodes.

"I think you made me strain my back, bendin' me over like that."

"I'm sure it'll heal fast," Rhodes said. He looked toward the driveway. "That's a nice-looking car you have under that tarp."

Overton glanced in the direction of the car. "That car belonged to my daddy. He loved that old car. Took good care of it right up till the day he died."

"I could tell it was in good shape," Rhodes said.

"It needs some body work and a new paint job. But one of the last things Daddy did after he put it up on the blocks was to drain the oil out of the crankcase and put the tires in storage. I still got those tires. Genuine wide white sidewalls on 'em."

Rhodes was impressed. "I don't suppose you'd like to sell the tires and car along with them."

"I wouldn't mind sellin' it, tires and all," Overton said. "It's just stuff that's takin' up room, and I'll never have the money to get it fixed up right."

Rhodes started to ask him how much he wanted for it.

He didn't get a chance, however, because Overton said, "But much as I'd like to get rid of it, I sure as hell wouldn't sell it to you."

TWELVE

A DISAPPOINTED RHODES was headed home when he got a call from Hack on the radio.

"Ty Berry's here at the jail," Hack told him. "Says he has to talk to you."

Rhodes had planned to go by his house, feed his dog, and maybe even have a quiet supper with Ivy. Well, he thought, he could still do all that if Berry didn't keep him too long.

"Tell him I'll be there in five minutes," he said, and turned the car toward the jail.

BERRY WAS SITTING by Rhodes's desk when the sheriff arrived. He stood up when Rhodes entered the room.

"I'm glad you could get here so soon," he said. He looked over at Hack, who was watching the early news on his little Sony. "Is there somewhere that we can talk?"

"We can talk right here," Rhodes told him. "Anything you can say to me, you can say in front of Hack."

Hack nodded, but said nothing, apparently intent on a story about an alligator that was caught crossing a highway down near Houston.

"All right, then," Berry said.

He sank back in the chair, and Rhodes walked over to his desk and sat down.

"What's the trouble?" Rhodes asked.

"I got a phone call a little while ago from someone who's not a member of the Clearview Historical Society but who knows a lot of them. He says there's a plot afoot to move the Burleson cabin to town tonight and put it in the city park."

Several questions immediately occurred to Rhodes. He asked the first one: "Why not the courthouse lawn?"

Berry pulled a wrinkled handkerchief from his shirt pocket, took off his Catamount cap, and wiped his balding head. He stuck the handkerchief back in his pocket and put his cap back on.

"If you think that was a hard question," Rhodes said, "how about this one: who called you?"

"I suppose I can tell you that. It was Mack Riley."

Rhodes knew Mack. He was a cranky old codger, too ornery to join either the Sons and Daughters of Texas or the Historical Society because neither of them would let him run the show. When he was younger, he had by all accounts been a real hellion, getting into one fight after another.

But age or wisdom or both had supposedly reformed him, and now the only fights he got into were fights that used words. He was a self-appointed expert on the history of Blacklin County and a frequent contributor to the Clearview *Herald*'s letters-to-the-editor column. His letters usually condemned either the Society or the Sons and Daughters for some misguided project or what Riley saw as a distortion of history in an article written by one of their members.

"Mack's on your side?" Rhodes said.

"This time he is," Berry said.

"Okay. I'll take your word for it. Now, tell me why the city park."

"Mack says it's because the county commissioners would never allow anyone to just set the cabin on the courthouse lawn and get away with it. They'd have it hauled off the next day."

Rhodes worked closely with the commissioners. They could be as cranky as Mack Riley when the occasion demanded it, and he didn't imagine they'd be any too happy to see the Burleson cabin parked on the courthouse lawn. Riley was probably right about their reaction.

"But the city council's different," Berry said. "Mack says they haven't done a thing for that park in years except let it to go to hell in a handbasket. They'll hardly even pay for someone to cut the weeds in the summer. If the Society puts the cabin there and promises to take care of the upkeep, maybe even keep up the whole park, the council will let them leave the cabin for as long as they want to."

That too sounded about right to Rhodes. The council would do just about anything to save money, even the little bit of money they spent on mowing the park two or three times a year.

"Where did Mack get his information?"

"He didn't say. But he knows a lot of people, and he's a good listener. People like to talk to him."

Rhodes figured that Berry would have mentioned the drowning to Riley, so he said, "Did Mack have anything to say about Yeldell?"

Berry took off his cap again, but he didn't wipe his head. He just put the cap on his knee and left it there.

"He thinks the same thing I do."

"What's that?"

"That it would be just like Faye Knape to put that rope in the tree and then suggest to Yeldell that he go swimming out there."

The rope's being tied to a rotten limb could be explained by the fact that someone wanted the limb to break, but Rhodes found it hard to believe that Faye Knape was that someone. And he didn't think that Faye and Pep Yeldell moved in the same social circles.

"Are you making an accusation?" he asked.

Berry looked down at his cap. "I don't know," he said.

"It seems pretty unlikely to me that Faye Knape would know someone like Pep Yeldell," Rhodes said. "And depending on a rotten limb to break and kill someone seems a whole lot more unlikely than that."

"It's not so unlikely if the someone was drunk. Yeldell liked to drink."

"Let me see if I've got this right," Rhodes said. "Faye Knape doesn't want the Old Settlers' Days to be a success, so she climbs one of the tallest pecan trees on the grounds. Then she ties a rope to a rotten limb in the hopes that some intoxicated man, or a woman would do, I guess, will come along, swing on the rope, get hit in the head by the falling limb, and drown in the pool.''

Hack made a sound that might have been a cough or a laugh, and Berry looked over in his direction. Hack was staring hard at a slick-haired anchorman and didn't appear to notice.

Berry turned back to Rhodes. "It sounds ridiculous when you say it that way, but it could have happened. And then there's Grat Bilson.''

Grat was the vice president of the Historical Society. He was a former Clearview Catamount football player now in his middle forties but still in commendable condition.

"What about him?" Rhodes asked.

"Well, he could climb that tree, for one thing.''

"Maybe," Rhodes admitted, "but it still sounds ridiculous.''

"How about this then," Berry said. "When Pep Yeldell was in high school, he stole Bilson's car.''

"Check on that, Hack," Rhodes said.

"Check on what?" Hack asked, as if he hadn't been listening to every word.

Rhodes told him, and Hack went to work on his computer. It didn't take long.

"Joyridin'," Hack said. "The car wasn't hurt.''

"But it gives Bilson a motive for murder," Berry said. "He's the kind of man who holds a grudge.''

Rhodes didn't agree. "It sounds pretty thin, and the method is still ridiculous.''

Berry took his cap off his knee, smoothed down what was left of his hair, and fitted the cap on his head.

"I don't think you care about Pep Yeldell," he said. "Or about the Burleson cabin."

"I don't know that there's much I can do about either one of them. Dr. White's autopsy report indicates that Yeldell died by accident. As for the cabin, I'm not sure that the Historical Society would be breaking any law by moving it."

Berry's face turned red. "How can you say that?"

Rhodes didn't answer; he asked another question. "Who owns the cabin?"

Berry opened his mouth, then shut it.

"Your bunch paid for the restoration," Rhodes said. "But that doesn't make you the owners. Do you have a deed to it?"

"Well, no, but that's not the point."

"What is the point, then?"

"The point is that they're going to move it!"

"Maybe they have a deed to it."

"They don't. They can't!"

"They might. Have you tried to find out?"

Berry stood up. "Sheriff, I hope you're not counting on my support in the next election. I could never vote for a man who won't uphold the law."

"I'm doing my best," Rhodes said.

"Well it's not good enough."

Berry stalked away, his shoulders rigid. He tried to slam the door, but it had an automatic closer on it.

"Looks like you lost a vote," Hack said, looking

at the door and no longer making a pretense of watching TV.

"It's not the first one," Rhodes said.

"Won't be the last one, either. You really gonna let them move that cabin to town?"

"We'll see," Rhodes said.

THIRTEEN

RHODES WAS ABOUT TO leave when Ruth Grady came in.

"I've been talking to Bull Lowery," she said.

Bull was the owner of Lowery's Paint and Body, where Pep Yeldell had worked.

"Dr. White seems to think Yeldell's death was an accident," Rhodes told her, describing what he'd read in the report. "Did Bull give you any reason to doubt any of that?"

"It's hard to say. Did you know that Bull was Yeldell's brother-in-law?"

Rhodes shook his head. "I didn't even know Yeldell was married. Hack?"

"See what I'm tellin' you about computers?" Hack said. "You gotta have 'em."

"Never mind the little lesson in life," Rhodes said. "Just check on Yeldell."

In a few seconds Hack said, "Married to Cissy Lowery in 1993, divorced the same year."

"It didn't last very long," Rhodes said.

"According to Bull, it lasted too long," Ruth said. "He says that Pep was an abuser."

"Hack?"

Hack pecked at the keyboard. "Nope. Not a single complaint."

"I didn't think I remembered one," Rhodes said. "She never reported him."

"There's nothing unusual in that," Ruth said.

Rhodes nodded. "The only unusual thing is that she left him. Usually abused women stay around way too long."

"Don't see why somebody'd hire a man who abused his sister," Hack said.

Ruth had asked about that. "He says that Yeldell was a good worker and that they kept things strictly business between them. As long as Yeldell wasn't anywhere near his sister, Bull didn't worry about him."

"He didn't mind him gettin' close to other women?" Hack asked.

"He didn't think that was any of his business," Ruth said.

Hack's head wagged. "Hard to account for the way some men think."

"Apparently he was keeping his act clean," Rhodes said. "We haven't had any complaints of that kind about him, and he's been going around with quite a few women if what Ruth heard earlier is the truth."

"Bull says it's true. Yeldell got around, all right. Sometimes men don't try anything like that on a woman until they've developed a really close relationship. Don't ask me why."

Rhodes didn't know either, but he knew she was right.

"Did he know anything about what Yeldell did last night?"

"He says Pep liked to go out to The County Line and have a few beers. If Pep didn't have a date, he could always meet someone out there."

There was nothing new in any of that. In view of the autopsy report, Rhodes wasn't sure that it was worth his while to investigate Yeldell's death any farther. But he still had that itch between his shoulder blades, that little intuition that kept telling him something was wrong. Maybe he'd go out to The County Line and ask a few questions.

"What about cars coming in for body work?" Rhodes asked. "Has Bull seen anything suspicious?"

"Like a Jeep Cherokee?" Ruth asked.

"Like that, or like a car that's dented on the front end from an unreported accident."

"I asked about that. But he says he hasn't seen a thing like that. Just the usual stuff."

"Figgers," Hack said. "I'm tellin' you, that Cherokee's over there in Russia right now. Prob'ly loaded with Levi's when they shipped it, too."

"You never can tell," Rhodes said.

RHODES DIDN'T get home in time to feed the dog or eat supper. He did manage a phone call, but that was it. Ivy said she'd take care of the dog and keep his supper warm.

"What's it going to be?" he asked.

"Vegetable soup. With cornbread."

"Low-fat cornbread, I guess," Rhodes said.

"As low as cornbread gets. We have to make up

for that bacon cheeseburger. Not to mention the Blizzard.''

"I might be late," Rhodes said.

"It won't be the first time, will it."

There was no reproach in the words, for which Rhodes was grateful.

"No," he said. "And it won't be the last."

"I knew what I was getting into when I married a man of action," Ivy told him. "So I don't mind. Much. Just be sure I get my share of the action."

"I promise."

"I'll hold you to it."

"I hope so," he said.

ONE REASON Rhodes didn't get home was that Hack got a call from a stranded motorist out on the highway about halfway to Thurston. The motorist said that he'd had a flat and was changing his tire when someone stopped on the shoulder of the road behind him. The motorist thought it was a Good Samaritan, stopping to help out.

"Only he didn't help," Hack reported straightforwardly. He had to be straightforward, since Rhodes had been listening to one side of the conversation. "He just grabbed up the guy's spare, which was a practically new Michelin radial lyin' there on the ground. He threw it in the back of his truck, got in, and took off."

"Did you get a description?" Rhodes asked.

"For a wonder," Hack said. "The guy that called is pretty bright. He says it was a red Isuzu, and he even got the license number."

"Run it," Rhodes said.

Hack did. "Jerry Grubbs. Well, we sure know him, don't we?"

"We sure do. He's probably at home right now, thinking about selling the tire."

Ruth was off duty, having already put in some overtime, and Buddy, the night deputy, was on patrol. Buddy could pick up the motorist. That left it to Rhodes to see about Grubbs.

Rhodes knew where Grubbs lived, since, as Hack said, they knew him. Grubbs had never worked for a living as far as Rhodes knew. He had always lived with his parents, who supported him until he was nearly thirty. Then his father died of a heart attack. His mother died of cancer a year later. Both of them had insurance, though not much, which seemed to be fine with Grubbs. He didn't need much, and what he couldn't afford to buy with the insurance money, he stole.

He never stole much that Rhodes knew about— beer at a convenience store, a pair of jeans at Wal-Mart, a car battery at John West's auto parts store, a package of Trojans from Billy Lee's drug store.

What Rhodes sometimes worried about was what didn't get reported. Grubbs had a habit of picking up anything he took a fancy to, and there were bound to have been times when he got away with things. People knew about him, and they were careful when he was around, but they couldn't watch him every single minute.

The truth was that Grubbs didn't really know better than to steal. He wasn't exactly the most intelligent resident of the county, and he had strange ideas about property. He'd never served more than a few days in jail because he was always sorry about having taken something that wasn't his. That is, he was sorry when things were explained to him. Sometimes it took a while for the message to get through. And when it finally did, he immediately forgot it.

Grubbs lived just off an unpaved county road in the run-down house his parents had left him. He hadn't taken care of the place, and even in the dark Rhodes could see that in a few years the area around the house would look more like a dump than a front yard.

The red Isuzu looked good, though. It was the only thing that Grubbs seemed to care about. It was parked at least twenty feet from the chinaberry tree that four or five scraggly white leghorns were roosting in.

Rhodes parked the county car and turned off the lights. By the time he got out, Grubbs had turned on the porch light and joined him in the yard.

"Hey, Sheriff," Grubbs said. "How ya doin'?"

He was short and wiry, and he wore jeans and a cowboy hat that pushed down on his ears because it was about one size too big. Rhodes wondered where he'd picked it up.

"I'm doing fine, Jerry. How are you?"

"Great. Great. Been watchin' a little TV. Sure some funny shows on these days, right?"

"I wouldn't know," Rhodes said. He never watched TV except when some old movie was on.

"Well, there are. The one about that nanny cracks me up. I love to hear her say 'Ohhhhhh, Mr. Sheffield.'"

Rhodes supposed that Grubbs was trying some kind of accent, but he couldn't figure out what it was.

"You haven't been watching TV all night, have you?" he asked.

"Whatcha mean, Sheriff?"

"I hear you've been helping out stranded motorists."

"Oh, yeah. That guy with the flat. I gave him a hand out there on the road."

"You didn't exactly give him a hand, Jerry. You took his spare tire."

Jerry appeared to be completely amazed. "Me?"

"You."

Jerry looked all around the yard. "I don't see any tire. Do you?"

"No," Rhodes said. "Where is it?"

"Where is what?"

"The tire, Jerry. I know you took it."

"Think you can find it?"

Rhodes couldn't see too much of the area around the house in the dim light from the porch. Besides, he didn't want to spend any time looking for something that Jerry could show him.

"I don't want to look for it, Jerry. Why don't you tell me where it is?"

"If you can't find it, I get to keep it, don't I?"

"That's not the way it works," Rhodes said.

"Finders, keepers; losers, weepers."

"That's not exactly the way the law reads," Rhodes said. "And you didn't find the tire."

Jerry jammed his hands in the back pockets of his jeans and looked stubborn.

"Did so find it," he said. "It was layin' right there in the road."

"The man who owns it was about to put it on his car."

"Well, he shoulda said so. Shouldn't have left it layin' there where somebody could just run over it."

"He didn't leave it lying there, Jerry. He took it out of his trunk so he could put it on his car."

"Well, it's mine now. Finders, keepers."

"No, Jerry. It still belongs to the man who was changing the tire. Where is it?"

"I'm not tellin'. If you find it, you can have it, though. That's fair. Finders, keepers."

Rhodes knew how to be patient, but he wasn't going to spend the night arguing with Jerry Grubbs.

"If you don't tell me where the tire is, I'm going to have to take you in to the jail, Jerry. I don't have time to look for it tonight."

Jerry stuck his hands deeper into his back pockets. "Finders, keepers."

"You won't change your mind?"

"Finders, keepers. Losers, weepers."

"All right, then. Let's go to the jail."

"Can I go turn off my TV?"

"Let's get you in the car," Rhodes said. "I'll turn off the TV for you."

"No, no!" Jerry shook his head violently and

turned to the house, breaking into a run before Rhodes could grab him. "No, no!"

Rhodes followed as fast as he could, stumbling on the hard, churned ground. He caught up with Jerry just inside the front door and saw at once why Jerry hadn't wanted him to turn off the TV. The tire was sitting there in the living room, right up on the couch as if it were watching *The Nanny*.

Jerry made a dive for it. "Finders, keepers!"

"Not this time, Jerry," Rhodes said, grabbing Grubbs's arm. "I'll just take that now."

Holding onto Grubbs, he walked over to the couch. "I'm going to let you go. Will you stand right there?"

"I guess so," Grubbs said. "I sure do like that tire, though. It's a Michelin."

"I think I'd better take it back to the owner," Rhodes said, letting go of Grubbs's arm. "He's not going to be too happy with you, but he might not press charges. If he does, I'll have to come back to see you tomorrow."

Grubbs was rubbing his arm. "I always like to have you come by for a visit, Sheriff."

Rhodes took the tire off the couch, bounced it on the floor, and rolled it to the door.

"Try to stay out of trouble, Jerry," he said.

"I always try to stay out of trouble. People just act crazy sometimes."

"I guess they do at that," Rhodes said.

RHODES DROVE BACK to the jail and picked up the motorist, whose name was Pat Grove. Then they drove to the stranded car, a Honda Accord.

Rhodes parked and put on his flashers, then helped Grove put on the spare. It didn't take long.

"Thanks for the help, Sheriff," Grove said when he'd put his tools back in the trunk and closed it. "That was pretty fast work."

"You gave a good description," Rhodes said.

"It was still fast. If I lived in this county, you'd get my vote for sure."

Rhodes smiled. "I could use it," he said.

FOURTEEN

THE OTHER REASON that Rhodes missed his supper was that after helping Pat Grove change the tire he decided to drive out to the Old Settlers' Grounds just to see if there was any truth in the rumor that Mack Riley had started.

As it turned out, there was.

Even before Rhodes arrived at the Grounds, he could see lights. They weren't moving, but it was obvious that they were headlights. When Rhodes drove under the arches over the gateway, he could see the cars and pickups parked all around the Burleson cabin.

And when he got closer, he could see trouble.

Ty Berry was on the porch of cabin, frozen in the glare of the headlights and holding what looked like an old over-and-under twelve-gauge shotgun. Members of the Clearview Historical Society and the Clearview Sons and Daughters of Texas surrounded the cabin and were pushing and shoving and yelling at one another. Rhodes picked out Faye Knape, Grat Bilson, and Grat's wife, Yvonne. Mack Riley was there, too, along with quite a few others that Rhodes didn't know.

A modified flatbed truck with a motorized winch up near the rear of the cab was backed up to the cabin. A ramp from the truck bed was shoved just under the front porch. The winch wasn't hooked to anything yet. The cable was still wrapped around the drum, and Ty Berry looked determined to make sure it stayed there.

Tuffy West stood in front of the truck away from the pushing and shoving. He was smoking a cigarette, completely unconcerned with what was happening.

Rhodes parked a good distance from the unruly crowd, got out of the county car, and walked over to where Tuffy was standing.

"Hey, Sheriff," Tuffy said.

No one else was paying any attention to Rhodes. Probably no one had even noticed him drive up. Everyone was too busy yelling at everyone else. Mack Riley was yelling louder than anyone, but no one seemed to be listening to him or to anyone else.

"What are you doing here, Tuffy?" Rhodes asked, speaking louder than he usually did so that Tuffy could hear.

Tuffy tossed his cigarette to the ground and mashed it out with the toe of his work boot.

"This here's my truck," he said, jerking his head backward as if to point it out. "I got paid to do a moving job, so here I am."

"You think that cabin would hold together if you tried winching it up on the truck bed with that cable?" Rhodes asked.

Tuffy shrugged. "Not my problem. Miz Knape asked me to move something, so I told her I'd try. I'm working by the hour, so the way I figure it, I get paid whether the cabin stays or goes."

"Did it ever occur to you that moving this cabin might be illegal?"

"Didn't figure it was any of my business one way or the other. I'm just the hired help here, tryin' to earn an honest dollar."

"And you say Mrs. Knape hired you?"

"That's right, but she said the Historical Society would pay me."

"I don't think you're going to get paid," Rhodes said. "This cabin's not going anywhere."

Tuffy shrugged again. "Like I said, I'm on the clock. I'm earnin' money right now, while they all holler at each other. If they don't want me to move the cabin, that's fine with me. I'll just take my truck and go home."

"Why don't you do that right now," Rhodes said. "You've probably made a good night's pay already."

Tuffy nodded, and went around to the side of the truck. Rhodes heard the door open, and Tuffy climbed inside. The door slammed shut.

The sound didn't register on the arguing crowd. Nobody noticed a thing until Tuffy started the truck, and even then only a couple of people were curious enough to turn around to see what the noise was all about.

Everyone noticed when Tuffy put the truck in gear and started to pull away, however. There were a few energetic cheers from the Sons and Daughters, and one or two outbursts of another kind from the members of the Historical Society as the truck rumbled away.

Then they all turned to each other and started yelling again. Grat Bilson was standing toe to toe with Mack Riley, and Faye Knape was yelling at both of them. Rhodes couldn't distinguish the words, but he started in their direction because he was afraid someone, most likely Mack, was going to get hurt if he didn't intercede.

He was too late, though. Mack threw a punch that surprised Bilson and glanced off his cheekbone.

Bilson didn't like getting hit. He had thirty years and at least fifty pounds on Riley, but that didn't prevent him from striking back. He hit Riley on the left shoulder with a short right, and aimed a roundhouse left for his head.

Riley might have been old, but he wasn't slow. He ducked to the right and kicked out at Bilson's knee with an old street fighter's move.

He couldn't kick as high as when he was a young man, so he missed the knee and connected with Bilson's shin, which probably hurt just as much. Maybe more, because Bilson bent over and grabbed at his leg, at which point Riley slammed a fist into the back of his head and laid him on the ground.

Suddenly it got very quiet, except for the high-pitched scream from Yvonne Bilson as she jumped on Riley's back and wrapped her legs around his waist. She started to pull his thin white hair with her left hand and pound his chest with her right, all the time keeping up a thin, wavery howl.

Faye Knape was trying to peel her off when Rhodes got there, and the sheriff let her finish the job. It would be better that way, and Faye looked up to it.

Riley fell to his hands and knees before Faye could get a good hold on Yvonne, but finally Faye was able to separate them. By then, there was no more arguing or yelling. Everyone was watching to see who would be attacked next, or whether Grat Bilson would be able to get up before Mack Riley, who was still down after Faye had dragged Yvonne to the cabin porch.

Ty Berry, noticing Rhodes's arrival, yelled, "It's about time you got here, Sheriff."

Everyone turned from looking at Bilson and Riley to stare at Rhodes.

"I warned you this was going to happen, Sheriff," Berry said. "But you didn't try to stop it. It's a wonder somebody hasn't been killed."

"That's always a danger when somebody's waving a shotgun around," Rhodes said. "Why don't you put it down, Ty."

Berry looked at the shotgun as if surprised to see it in his hands. Then he leaned it against the cabin door.

"That's better," Rhodes said. "Now, somebody see about Mack and Grat and then tell me what's going on here."

Mack was already standing, glaring in the direction of Yvonne Bilson, a skinny blonde who didn't really look heavy enough to have borne him down. Two men were helping Grat to his feet, and he was shaking his head as if to clear it.

"Who wants to start?" Rhodes said, looking from one to another of them. "How about you, Ty?"

"Well, it's clear as day," Berry said. "I warned you, but you wouldn't listen to me. These Society fools are out here trying to hijack the cabin and haul it into town. And we came out here to stop 'em."

"We're not hijacking anything," Faye Knape said.

She was even taller than Yvonne Bilson, and her hair was very black, unnaturally so. She wasn't married, and lived in a house filled with cats of all sizes and colors. Rhodes didn't know how many cats she had. No one else did, either. Probably even Faye wasn't sure.

"You are so hijacking something," Berry said, and the arguing broke out again.

"Hold it!" Rhodes yelled, and everyone got quiet. "Let's try to talk one at a time. Just exactly what were you trying to do, Mrs. Knape?"

"We were going to take the cabin into Clearview where it belongs," she said. "And we have a perfect right to do it."

"That's a lie!" Berry said. "You don't have any more right to it than a 'possum!"

"Oh, yes, we do," Faye said. "And if you'd just listen to me, I could prove it to you."

"That's another lie," Berry said. "Don't let her get away with it, Sheriff. Arrest her!"

"I can't arrest anyone for lying," Rhodes said. "If she is lying."

"I'm not," Faye said. "Just let me get my purse."

She started toward a car, and Berry said, "Don't let her, Sheriff! She might be going for a gun!"

"The only gun I see out here is yours," Rhodes told him. "And I can arrest you for that a lot quicker than I can arrest someone for lying."

"I didn't shoot anybody."

"No, but I expect a lot of these people here would swear that you threatened them. To the law, that's almost as bad as shooting them."

Berry didn't have anything to say to that, so he shut up.

Faye Knape slammed her car door and came back to Rhodes with a piece of paper in her hand.

"This is a letter of permission to move the Burleson cabin," she said, waving the paper in the air.

"Bullcorn!" Ty Berry said. "It's no such thing."

"Yes, it is," Faye said. "Signed by the heirs."

"That's another lie," Ty said. "There aren't any heirs."

"You're wrong about that," Faye said. "As you'd know if you ever took the time to do any research. The Historical Society does its research before making any moves, and we found the heirs." She handed the paper to Rhodes. "You can read all about it."

Rhodes looked at the paper. He couldn't read it, not without his glasses, which he didn't want to put on at the moment, and not in the dim light from the car headlights.

"I'll take it with me and read it at the office," he said. "Right now, I think everyone should go on home until this is all straightened out."

"I'm not going anywhere," Ty Berry said. "If I do, they'll try to steal the cabin again."

"No, they won't. I'll see to that."

Faye looked as if she might want to argue, but she didn't. No one else did, either. Rhodes's arrival had put a damper on their enthusiasm. The crowd began to break up, and people headed for their cars.

"Are you going to be all right, Mack?" Rhodes asked Riley.

Riley massaged his chest where Yvonne had pounded him, then touched the scratches on his head.

"I'll live, I guess," he said. "She never would've got me down if she'd come at me from the front."

"What about you, Grat?" Rhodes asked.

"Riley assaulted me," Bilson said. "I think you should arrest him."

"I didn't hit you till you called me a son of a bitch," Mack said. "You're the one oughta be arrested."

"Nobody's being arrested," Rhodes said. "I don't think there's any need for anyone to file charges about this." He looked around at the thinning crowd. "Just get yourselves home and forget about it."

"Some things you can't forget, Sheriff," Ty Berry said. "Like when your wife's been running around on you with the guy who stole your car."

Yvonne Bilson turned toward the cabin. "You son of a bitch," she said.

"Like husband, like wife," Berry said.

"Let's all settle down now," Rhodes said.

"Maybe the Bilsons had better stay here for a minute. You, too, Ty."

"I'll stay, too," Faye Knape said.

"I don't think so," Rhodes told her. "You can go on home. Come by the jail tomorrow and we can talk this over."

"I'll take my letter with me, then."

"I think I'd better hold onto it, just in case," Rhodes said.

Faye obviously didn't like it, but she refrained from saying so.

"Don't let him intimidate you," she told Bilson.

"You don't have to worry about *that*," Yvonne said, and Rhodes had no trouble at all believing her.

FIFTEEN

WHEN THE CARS were gone, it was much darker. There was only a sliver of moon, and dust hung in the air and tickled Rhodes's nose.

"Now, then, Ty, why don't you explain what you were talking about a while ago," Rhodes said.

He and Berry were sitting on the edge of the porch. The shotgun was safely stowed in the cab of Berry's truck, and the Bilsons stood a few feet away, scowling.

"It's like I was saying," Berry began, but Yvonne interrupted.

"Don't listen to him. He's a liar from the word go."

"I can find out easily enough," Rhodes said. "If not from him, from somebody else. Go ahead, Ty."

"Well, there's not all that much to tell. Pep Yeldell stole Grat's car a while back, like I told you at the jail. And later on he was trying to steal his wife, too."

"You son of a bitch," Yvonne said.

"The curse of a limited vocabulary," Ty said, shaking his head. "But it's the truth, Sheriff. You can ask around."

"Why should he?" Grat asked. "It's all in the past. It doesn't mean a thing."

"It's a motive for murder," Berry said. "That's what it is."

Bilson started for Berry. Rhodes slid off the porch and stood between them.

"You've already lost one fight tonight," he told Bilson. "Don't start another one."

"I'm not starting anything. That little weasel is starting it, by lying about my wife."

"Is it a lie?" Rhodes asked, looking at Yvonne.

"It sure is," she said. "Pep and I might have gone out a time or two, but I was just mad at Grat when I did it, and I was trying to get back at him. I got over my mad, and everything was all right."

"When was this?" Rhodes asked.

"A long time ago," Yvonne said.

"How long?"

Yvonne waved a hand in the air. "A month or so. I don't really remember."

"Try," Rhodes said.

"What difference does it make?" Grat asked. "I didn't kill anybody, much less Pep Yeldell. I heard he drowned while he was swimming out here. That sounds like an accident to me."

"Not if somebody tried to make him swing on that rope," Berry said.

"Don't start that again," Rhodes warned him, realizing just how far-fetched Berry's theory had been in the first place.

"Did you know John West?" he asked Bilson.

"Who?"

"He was killed in a hit-and-run accident about two and a half weeks ago," Rhodes said.

"I heard about the accident," Bilson said. "I never met West, though."

"What's that got to do with anything?" Berry asked.

"Probably nothing," Rhodes said, looking at Yvonne, who seemed about to say something.

She didn't, however. She went over to the porch and sat down.

"This is stupid," Bilson said. "I'm not going to stay out here any more and listen to Ty Berry call me a murderer. I never killed anybody, and I'm going home. Come on, Yvonne."

Yvonne joined him, and they started for their car. Rhodes didn't try to stop them.

"Are you just going to let them leave?" Berry asked.

"Yes," Rhodes said. "Pep Yeldell might have gone joyriding in Bilson's car, and he might have fooled around with Yvonne a little, but Dr. White says he most likely died by accident. Let's just leave it that way for now."

"I guess you know you've lost my vote," Berry said.

"You told me that already."

"I just thought I'd remind you," Berry said.

THE THIRD THING that kept Rhodes from getting home was a sermon. It was Wednesday night, and Brother Alton had held his usual midweek services. It was the sermon that was unusual. Rhodes heard about it from Randall Overton when he stopped by the jail later that evening.

"He called down the wrath of God on me," Overton said. "Right up there from the pulpit. He said that the earth would swallow me up and the fires of hell would consume me."

"Did he yell when he said it?" Hack asked. "I like a preacher that can yell a little. I like one that can cry a little, too, when he tells a sad story. What about you, Sheriff?"

"I don't like yelling," Rhodes said. "How do you know about this, Mr. Overton?"

Overton was still wearing his Joe Camel T-shirt. He didn't look as if he'd been to church.

"Somebody phoned me," he said. "So I don't know about any yelling. And I don't care whether he yelled or not. I want you to go to that church and arrest him."

Rhodes thought for a minute. Brother Alton wanted Overton arrested for fraud, Ty Berry wanted Faye Knape arrested for lying, and now Overton wanted Brother Alton arrested for preaching a sermon. Rhodes wondered if it wasn't time for him to consider moving to somewhere quieter and less stressful—somewhere like, say, New York City.

"He was making a threat against me," Overton said to help Rhodes along with his decision-making.

"He was just preachin'," Hack said. "Usin' you as an example, you might say. Can't arrest a man for that."

"I wasn't talking to you," Overton said. "I was talkin' to the sheriff."

Hack's mouth drew itself into a tight line. Rhodes felt sorry for Overton if he ever did have to spend any time in the Blacklin County jail. Hack would probably do something to his food.

"Hack's right," Rhodes said, both to pacify his dispatcher and because it was the truth. "There's no law in preaching against a man. But I'll talk to Brother Alton and tell him that you're going to take care of the roof. That ought to satisfy him. I don't think you'll have to worry about him preaching about you again."

"He'd better not," Overton said. "Not if he knows what's good for him."

"Now *that's* a threat," Hack said. "What you said's not like talkin' about a man in a sermon. It's what we call a terroristic threat. You can get yourself arrested for that. 'Course I'm not the sheriff. *I* can't arrest you."

"And I'm not going to," Rhodes said. "Not this time. But don't make any more threats. And fix that roof."

Overton grumbled for a few seconds, but he left without making any trouble.

"I wish you'd locked him up," Hack said when the door shut behind Overton. "I'd like to help clean out his cell."

"I'll bet you would," Rhodes said. "But you won't get the chance."

"You never can tell," Hack said. "He looks like the type that'll be back this way sooner or later."

He didn't come back to the jail, however.

The next time Rhodes saw him, he was sitting behind the steering wheel of his shiny Toyota. The outside of the pickup was still in pretty good shape, which was more than you could say for Overton.

He was burned to crisp.

SIXTEEN

GERRI VESTAL and her ten-year-old son Harold found Overton early on Saturday morning, three days after Brother Alton's sermon had condemned Overton to be consumed by flames.

Rhodes had more or less put Overton out of his mind in the interim. He'd had other things to occupy his time, such as his meeting with Faye Knape.

The letter that she had produced seemed to be genuine, but just to be sure, Rhodes had called the brother and sister who signed it. They lived in a nursing home in south Texas, and they said that they had indeed written the letter. They also said they would be glad to send positive proof of their descent from Cletus Burleson.

"I told you the letter was genuine," Faye Knape said when Rhodes told her. "There was no need for you to call them. I could have provided you with the proper genealogical information if you'd just asked. As I told Mr. Berry, we in the Historical Society do our research thoroughly."

"I had to check," Rhodes said. "It's part of the job."

Faye Knape sniffed. Rhodes could see cat hairs on her blouse, and he wondered if she were allergic to her cats.

"Very well," she said. "You checked, and you

found out I was right. The descendants of Cletus Burleson, the legal heirs to the cabin, have given their permission to move it. I'm sure that settles everything to your satisfaction, and I hope you won't interfere again."

"I don't know about interfering," Rhodes said, "but I don't think I can let you go out there and move the cabin just yet. I told the Burleson heirs a few things that I haven't discussed with you yet."

Faye arched a very black eyebrow. "Who asked you to tell them anything?"

"Nobody," Rhodes said. "But it seemed like a good idea."

"What did you tell them?"

"Just a few things I thought maybe they didn't know about. It turns out that you didn't tell them the whole story about the cabin."

"I told them everything I thought they needed to know. They're getting on in years, and I was afraid that if I told them too much, it might just confuse them."

"I don't think Ty Berry would agree with you on that," Rhodes said. "Anyway, they didn't get confused at all."

Mrs. Knape sniffed again, but she didn't say anything.

Rhodes continued. "You didn't mention that the Sons and Daughters of Texas had paid for the cabin's restoration and had seen to it that it got taken care of."

"Out at the Old Settlers' Grounds. It doesn't belong there, and the heirs agreed."

"That was before they knew about what had been done. Somehow they got the impression that the cabin was in a pretty run-down condition and that no one was looking after it."

Faye inspected the floor for a while, and then she looked up at the ceiling. There wasn't much to see up there except a spider web up high in one of the corners where Lawton couldn't reach with his broom.

"I'm sure I don't know how they could have gotten that idea," Faye said finally.

"Me neither," Rhodes said. "But when I told them about the restoration and about the big celebration this summer, they seemed to think the best thing to do would be to leave the cabin where it is."

Faye drew herself up straight. "I hope you're not counting on the votes of any Historical Society members in the next election, Sheriff."

"When you think about it," Rhodes said as if he hadn't heard her, "the Grounds are the best place for the cabin. If you brought it to town and put it in the park, more people might see it, but it wouldn't be much of a tourist attraction. It's just a one-room cabin with nothing special about it."

"It's special to the Historical Society."

"Then you should get together with Ty Berry and see what you can do to help with the celebration next summer. As it stands now, the cabin gives people one more reason to drive out to the Old Settlers' Grounds. If your two groups worked together, we could have something really nice for the county."

"Ty Berry's planning to have Indian dances,"

Faye said. "There's already been talk of trouble about that."

"Maybe you could help him work it out so there wouldn't be any trouble. I imagine a woman with your ability to get along with people could work something out with Brother Alton."

"Well, maybe, but I don't think I can work with Ty Berry on *anything*."

"Why don't you give it a try? You might be surprised. Remember, his bunch cares just as much about that cabin and about the county's history as you and your group."

"Very well," Faye said. "I'll think about it. But I'm not making any promises. And I'm still not going to vote for you."

WHEN SHE LEFT, Hack said, "I really liked that part about her ability to get along with people. That was a good 'un."

"I thought you were watching that TV set."

"I can watch and listen at the same time. Besides, there's nothin' to see on Saturday mornin' except cartoons."

"I thought you liked cartoons."

"I like *The Tick,* but that's about it. And that's not on yet."

"The Tick?"

"Yeah."

Hack started to tell him about the show, but Rhodes didn't get the details. That was when Mrs. Vestal walked in.

MRS. VESTAL lived out on a little-traveled county road near Milsby, and she told Rhodes that she and Harold were driving into Clearview to do the weekly grocery shopping. They saw a red Toyota truck nosed into a ditch, and Harold yelled that he could see someone inside. Mrs. Vestal pulled over to the side of the road and got out of her car, telling Harold to stay where he was while she took a look.

"He didn't stay, though," she said, giving Harold a frown. "I oughta pinch his head off."

"It was gross," Harold said. "I wish I *had* stayed in the car. It smelled funny, too."

Harold had obviously been very impressed by what he'd seen, and so had Gerri Vestal. Rhodes took notes on the rest of their account and then sent them on to do their shopping, telling them that he would be in touch if he needed any further information.

"Can I go back in the jail and see the cells?" Harold asked.

Rhodes was about to tell him that he could, when Mrs. Vestal said, "Not today, Harold. We have to get the shopping done before noon. Your father will be expecting lunch."

"Come back some other time," Rhodes said. "I'll give you the guided tour."

"Can I?" Harold asked his mother.

"Maybe next Saturday," she said. "I'm sure it's quite educational."

Rhodes had never thought of it that way, but he said, "It sure is."

SEVENTEEN

RHODES DROVE OUT to where the Toyota truck sat in the ditch. The day was bright with sun, but there was a thick purple cloud bank massing in the direction of Dallas, a sure sign that a blue norther was on the way. Rhodes knew that when the wind hit, the sky would darken and the temperature would drop far and fast. It might even rain, but he hoped not.

He recognized the Toyota immediately as the one he'd seen in Randall Overton's driveway. Overton himself wasn't quite so easy to identify, though there was a tiny bit of the Joe Camel T-shirt left intact.

No one else had passed by since Mrs. Vestal, or if they had passed they hadn't been curious enough to stop and look. There was no sign that anyone had touched the truck or disturbed the area around it.

Rhodes called Hack and asked him to send Ruth Grady to meet him. He wanted all the help he could get in going over the scene, and he didn't want any mistakes.

"SO WHAT do you think?" Ruth asked a couple of hours later when they had completed their investigation. "Spontaneous combustion?"

The norther had hit while they were doing their

work. The sky was black and the wind was whistling through the barbed wire of the fence across the ditch. There was no rain, but the temperature had already dropped into the low forties. Rhodes was glad that he'd been carrying a coat in the car.

"You've been hanging around Hack too long," he told Ruth. "That's exactly what he said before I left the jail."

"He didn't mean it, though, did he?"

"No more than you did. What do you really think?"

"I think we've got something that looks a lot like another accident."

"It's not an accident," Rhodes said. "Not this time, for sure."

"I don't think so, either," Ruth said. "I said it *looks* like an accident. And somebody went to a lot of trouble to make it look that way. I might even believe it *was* an accident if it weren't for—"

"For the others," Rhodes said, finishing her sentence for her. "You can stretch coincidences only so far. This wasn't any accident."

There were two empty whiskey bottles in the Toyota, one in the floor and one in the seat beside Overton. The whole truck stank of liquor. It was supposed to appear that Overton had been drinking heavily and had pulled off the road, either because he realized that he was too drunk to drive or because he wanted a smoke.

There was an empty Camel filters package in the floor of the truck not far from the whiskey bottle. Overton had been drunk, had spilled whiskey all over himself, and had tried to smoke a cigarette. Either the flame from the butane lighter that was also in the floor had ignited the alcohol fumes or the cigarette had done that. Or that was what someone wanted Rhodes to think.

Overton had been too drunk to get out of the truck or even to open a door or window. He hadn't really burned to death, or at least Rhodes didn't think he had. It was more likely that he'd suffocated, but it would take the autopsy to prove it.

Either way, his death had been highly unpleasant.

And it could even have been an accident.

But Rhodes didn't believe it for a minute. He could accept a hit-and-run. Things like that happened now and then. And people drowned, too. People probably even caught on fire in their cars and either burned to death or suffocated.

But not in Blacklin County, not within weeks and days of one another. Something was going on, and Rhodes was going to find out what it was.

He didn't know exactly how, but he was determined that he was going to do it, one way or the other.

HE STARTED WITH Kara West, who once again asked if he had come with news about her husband.

"I'm afraid not," Rhodes said. "There's been another accident."

He told her about Overton, whom she professed never to have heard of until the previous Wednesday evening.

"So you heard Brother Alton's sermon," Rhodes said.

"No. I don't usually go to church on Wednesday. But someone told me about it. I knew that there had been some problems with the roof, of course. Surely you don't think Brother Alton had anything to do with this, do you? He's a minister of the gospel."

Rhodes had known a minister or two that he thought might be capable of murder, and he'd once had a personal tussle with Brother Alton, who'd jumped on him from a tree. You could never be sure what the preacher might do. But there was no need to mention that to Mrs. West.

"What about your husband?" Rhodes asked. "Did he know Overton?"

"I just don't have any idea. He might have known him. Maybe he bought some auto parts from John. I didn't spend much time at the store."

"And you never had any roofing done?"

"Never. We bought this house five years ago, and the roof had just been replaced. I don't know who did the work."

Rhodes didn't suppose it mattered. Kara West didn't appear to have any connection with either Yeldell or Overton. He told her that he would let her know as soon as he found out anything new about her husband's death and left to visit the Free Will Church.

BROTHER ALTON was sitting in his office, reading his Bible.

"The judgment of the Lord is swift and sure," he

said when Rhodes came in. "I told you that God would provide a judgment for Mr. Overton if you didn't."

"I remember that," Rhodes said. "And you told me that you'd help me and my deputies to see that no liquor was brought into the Old Settlers' Grounds during the celebration. What I'm wondering now is whether you helped God bring about that judgment on Randall Overton."

Brother Alton closed his Bible. "The Lord works in mysterious ways."

"You said that before, too," Rhodes reminded him. "But did you help Him out?"

"I am a servant of the Lord," Brother Alton said. "And the commandment says, 'Thou shalt not kill.'"

"And you wouldn't break a commandment."

"I didn't say that. Man is a weak reed, even a man devoted to the work of the Lord. But the story I heard was that Mr. Overton died by accident. Don't people call accidents 'acts of God'?"

"I don't," Rhodes said. "And I don't believe it was an accident."

"I'm sorry you're suspicious of me, Sheriff. I admit that I've given you cause in the past, but I've repented of my sins and confessed them to my flock."

"That's not all you've been talking to your flock about. I'd hate to find out that one of your members got it in mind to kill Overton after listening to your sermon last Wednesday night."

"I didn't tell them anything but the truth."

"What exactly did you say, anyway?"

"I said that Randall Overton had robbed the church and that robbing the church was an affront to God."

"And that's all you said?"

"I might have said a bit more. I don't remember."

"Let me help you out. You called down the fire on him, didn't you?"

"I might have said something about fire," Brother Alton admitted. "But if you think that I or someone in the church killed Mr. Overton, you're forgetting your own good influence on him."

"You mean my little talk with him did some good?"

"That's right. He came by on Thursday to say that he was going to finish the repairs this weekend. He especially asked me to let you know that he'd been here and that he was going to do the job."

"Why didn't you?"

"Because he hadn't done it yet." Brother Alton raised his eyes, either to the roof or to heaven. Then he looked back at Rhodes. "And now I guess he never will."

EIGHTEEN

IT WAS GETTING ON toward the middle of the afternoon when Rhodes left Brother Alton, and Rhodes had missed lunch again. He thought about stopping by the Dairy Queen for a Blizzard, but he knew that if he did he'd feel guilty for the rest of the afternoon. So instead he went by his house and ate a sandwich made of low-fat cheese and turkey bologna.

Rhodes supposed that turkey bologna was really just as tasty as the real thing to most people. It probably tasted like its plastic packaging to him only because he knew it was made of turkey instead of pork lips, or whatever it was that they put into real bologna. At least there was real Dr Pepper to wash it down with.

When he had finished eating, Rhodes tidied up the kitchen and went outside to see how his dog, Speedo, was doing. The cold wind was moaning through the nearly bare limbs of the pecan trees in Rhodes's yard, and dry leaves were blowing everywhere. Rhodes hoped they'd all blow into his neighbor's yard. Raking leaves wasn't one of his favorite pastimes.

Speedo was glad to see Rhodes, and unlike most humans Rhodes knew, Speedo didn't mind so much when the north wind blew and the weather turned cold. In fact, he enjoyed the cold. He dashed around the yard for a few seconds and then brought Rhodes an old yellow squeeze toy that he liked to play with. He dropped it at Rhodes's feet and looked at him hopefully.

Rhodes had taken the whistle out of the toy, which was shaped like a frog, so Speedo wouldn't accidentally choke on it, but Speedo didn't seem to miss the whistle. He liked the toy anyway.

Rhodes threw the rubber frog, and Speedo charged off after it. He overran it, skidded to a stop, spun around, and grabbed the toy in his mouth. Instead of taking it to Rhodes, however, he put it on the ground between his front legs and waited expectantly.

Rhodes walked over slowly, as if he had nothing better to do. Speedo wasn't fooled. His eyes followed Rhodes's every move.

Rhodes pretended to be completely uninterested in the frog. He looked up at the bare trees and the dark sky, then turned away. Speedo remained frozen in place, and Rhodes quickly turned back, bending down and reaching for the toy.

Just before Rhodes's fingers touched it, Speedo snatched it up and ran for the other side of the yard. When he got there, he put the frog down on the grass and waited. Rhodes obliged him, and they went through the entire routine again.

And again. After about ten minutes of the game, Rhodes was getting tired. Not Speedo. He would have kept it up all day if Rhodes had been willing.

Rhodes rubbed the dog's head and went to sit on the back steps where he could be out of the wind.

Speedo, knowing that the game was over, left the frog in the grass and came over to sit by Rhodes.

"What do you think, Speedo?" Rhodes said.

Speedo, who apparently found the question a little vague, kept quiet.

"Here's the thing," Rhodes said. "We have three accidents. Or that's what they seem like. The hit-and-run, that's a crime for sure. The other two aren't so easy to figure."

Speedo looked at Rhodes and gave a friendly growl.

"That's what I think, too," Rhodes said. "There's no reason why there has to be a connection between one or the other of them, but I think there is one. I think somebody killed all three of those men."

Speedo didn't comment. He got up and walked over to his food bowl and nosed around in it. There wasn't much there, but he ate what he could find. Then he went to his water dish and started lapping noisily.

"I don't even know if it's the same somebody," Rhodes said. "It could be that somebody read about the hit-and-run and then decided to kill the other people and make the killings look like accidents."

Speedo came back to the steps and sat down. He put his head on Rhodes's knee.

"What would you do if you were me?" Rhodes asked, rubbing Speedo's head.

Speedo wagged his tail. It lashed against Rhodes's ankle and against the step.

"I don't think wagging my tail would help," Rhodes said. "But thanks for the advice."

RHODES DECIDED to take a look at Overton's house. Maybe there would be something there that would give Rhodes a place to start. He also wanted to check on the dog he'd heard barking. He didn't want it to go hungry or mess up the house. And then there was the Edsel....

There was a gray Ford Tempo parked in Overton's driveway, so Rhodes went to the door and knocked. The dog started barking, and a heavyset woman with graying hair came to the door. Her eyes were red, as if she might have been crying.

Rhodes told her who he was, and she said that she was Alma Burkett, Overton's sister. Rhodes would have guessed that. Her face was flat, like her brother's, though her nose was more prominent. Rhodes had asked Ruth Grady to get in touch with the sister, who was Overton's only living relative, as far as Hack could discover.

"Have you talked to my deputy?" Rhodes asked, just to be sure.

"Yes. She came by the house. I thought I should come over here and see if there was anything I could do."

Rhodes looked over her shoulder into the dim interior of the house. He still couldn't see the dog, which had stopped barking.

"I wonder if I could come in," he said.

"The house is a mess. Randy wasn't a very neat person."

It was a mild shock to hear her call Overton *Randy*. It was hard for Rhodes to imagine a man like Overton having a nickname.

"I don't mind a little mess," Rhodes said. "I'd like to look around, see if there's anything that might help me in my investigation."

"Your deputy said that Randy had died in an accident."

"It might have been an accident," Rhodes said. The wind was blowing through his pants legs as if they were made of cheesecloth. "Or it might not. Could I come in?"

Mrs. Burkett moved aside, and Rhodes stepped into the house. He didn't have to go far to realize that Mrs. Burkett hadn't been exaggerating: Overton wasn't a very neat person.

There were newspapers on the floor, and there were socks and undershirts scattered here and there. Some were on the floor, and some were in chairs and on the couch. Rhodes smelled the strong odor of stale cigarette smoke mingled with the unpleasant aroma of unwashed clothes.

"I wish I could help you," Mrs. Burkett said. "But I don't know what it is that you're looking for."

Rhodes wasn't sure, either. But he said, "Business records. Did, uh, Randy keep accounts or tax records?"

Looking at the living room, Rhodes didn't have much hope of finding anything. If Overton kept records at all, they were most likely in complete disarray.

"He had a little bedroom that he used for an office," Mrs. Burkett said. "It's right over there."

She pointed at a door that was half open, and Rhodes started toward it. When he reached it, he pushed it open, and a dog charged out, yelping in what was no doubt supposed to be a threatening manner. It was hard for a dog that looked like a dust mop to be threatening, however, and Rhodes laughed aloud.

"It's just Yancey," Mrs. Burkett said. "He's a Pomeranian. He won't hurt you."

"I didn't think he would," Rhodes said, as the dog sank its teeth into the bottom of his pants leg and wagged its head from side to side, growling viciously, or as viciously as it could with a mouth full of cloth.

"You stop that, Yancey," Mrs. Burkett said. "I'm sorry, Sheriff. He just doesn't like strangers. I don't know what I'm going to do with him now that Randy's gone."

Yancey let go of Rhodes's pants, barked, and ran back into the office.

"You could take him home with you," Rhodes said. "He doesn't look like he'd eat a lot."

"Oh, I could never take him home. My husband, his name's Walter but everyone calls him Wally, he doesn't like dogs. He doesn't like cats, either. He doesn't like any animals at all. He won't have them around. I'll have to take Yancey to the pound."

Rhodes didn't much care for that idea. The pound was clean and well managed, and there were quite a few kindhearted people in Clearview, but it was by no means a certainty that someone would adopt Yancey.

"Don't you have any friends who'd like to have him? He's a feisty little guy."

"I'm afraid not. Most of the people I know have pets already, and the ones who don't wouldn't want one."

"Give it some thought while I see what's in the office," Rhodes said. "Maybe you can think of somebody. Or maybe your husband would know someone."

"Wally wouldn't want to be bothered. He just doesn't like animals at all, and he won't care what happens to Yancey. One reason he and Randy didn't get along was because of Yancey."

"Your husband didn't get along with Randy?"

"No. When I called and told him Randy was dead, he didn't shed a tear."

"Where does he work?"

"He drives a truck for Franklin Brothers. This is his week out of town."

"Oh," Rhodes said.

That let out Wally as a suspect. Franklin Brothers was a big wholesale beer distributor, and their drivers went practically all over the state.

Rhodes pushed open the door to Overton's office.

"If you need any help with Yancey, just call me," Mrs. Burkett said.

Rhodes didn't think he'd need any help. What could a Pomeranian do to him, after all?

NINETEEN

A POMERANIAN COULD surge out from under a desk and try to bite a hole in Rhodes's ankle, for one thing.

Rhodes shook the dog off before he destroyed a sock and turned on the light in the room.

The mess was worse than he had expected, and the smell of stale smoke was much stronger than it had been in the other room. There was a small desk littered with papers and magazines, and an overflowing ashtray sat on top of a *Playboy*. There were papers on the floor, too, and in the chair at the desk. Rhodes wondered where Overton sat. Probably on top of the papers.

Rhodes picked up some of the papers and looked at them while Yancey stood four or five feet away, barking at him.

"Hush, Yancey," Rhodes said.

To his surprise, Yancey did just that. The dog walked over to the corner, where something that might once have been a towel lay in a mangled yellow heap. Yancey walked around on the fabric a couple of times and then lay down, his paws stretched out in front of him and his eyes on Rhodes.

The papers that Rhodes had picked up weren't of any interest. They consisted of form letters asking if Overton wanted gold credit cards ("No Annual

Fee, Ever!''), offers to put siding on his house if he would allow the company to use the house as a "demonstrator" for the rest of the neighborhood, proposals to lend Overton money by mail ("No Credit Check!"), and attempts to sell Overton insurance—term life insurance, automobile insurance, hospitalization, worker's compensation, and even Medicare supplements. Overton hadn't been nearly old enough to worry about Medicare, but that didn't bother the direct mailers.

Rhodes put the form letters back on the desk. He wondered what kind of person kept things like that. Rhodes received much the same kind of mail practically every day, both at home and at his office, but it always went directly into the trash can, sometimes without being opened. Overton must never have thrown anything away. There wasn't even a trash can in the room as far as Rhodes could see.

Moving the ashtray, Rhodes picked up the *Playboy*. June 1993. Maybe there was a whole collection of *Playboy*s somewhere in the house, or maybe this was the only issue that Overton had ever bought. Rhodes started to put the magazine down when he saw the red corner of a spiral notebook sticking out from under a copy of *Texas Monthly*.

Rhodes pulled out the ledger book and put the *Playboy* in the chair. Then he opened the notebook and flipped through the pages. Each page was headed with the name of one of Overton's customers, and there was an accounting, written in pencil in an awkward scrawl, of what Overton had received

from each one of them, along with a record of the
materials he had bought for each job.

Overton had cheated Brother Alton's church, all
right. The evidence was right there. And he'd
cheated a lot of other people, too. Some more than
others.

There were several names and amounts that interested Rhodes more than the others.

Grat Bilson. Unless Overton had done magnificent work for him, something that Rhodes doubted
very much, Bilson had been cheated out of more
than two thousand dollars on a room remodeling job.

Mack Riley. He'd been cheated out of nearly nine
hundred dollars on an interior painting job. Of
course there was Overton's labor to figure in, but
nine hundred dollars to paint two rooms and a hall
seemed excessive.

Bull Lowery. Overton had charged him five thousand dollars to roof his house. As far as Rhodes
could see, Overton hadn't bought enough shingles
to roof a room, much less an entire house. But
maybe Overton's records were as sloppy as his
housekeeping.

Ty Berry. Overton had remodeled his kitchen at
a cost of four thousand dollars.

There were plenty of other names, but those were
the interesting ones. Three of them were connected
in one way or another to the Old Settlers' Grounds
where Yeldell had died, and the other was Yeldell's
boss.

The records went back over nearly three years. In
every case, Overton had spent next to nothing on his

materials, buying the cheapest available and usually not buying enough to complete the job. And if the way he kept up his own house was any indication, he wasn't really capable of doing the work he'd been hired to perform.

Rhodes had dealt with people like Overton before. They weren't basically dishonest. They advertised in the newspaper that they did handyman jobs, and when someone called and asked if they could re-model a kitchen or put on a roof, they said "Sure," because they needed the work and because they didn't think it would be too hard.

Later, when they saw that they'd gotten in over their heads, they always promised to make things right. And sometimes they actually tried to do that, time after time, but they simply couldn't, either out of incompetence or laziness or both. So they quit answering their telephones or went off to East Texas for a few weeks to stay with relatives. Eventually the people who had hired them gave up and found someone else to do the work and do it right.

They rarely came to the sheriff because they knew he wouldn't be able to do anything, not really. It was pretty much like Brother Alton had said. Getting a judgment against a deadbeat didn't mean anything if the deadbeat couldn't pay. Having him arrested for a misdemeanor like deceptive business practices didn't help matters, either. So they accepted their losses and chalked them up to experience.

Usually. Now and then things got a little out of hand. Someone would catch the deadbeat in the

Wal-Mart parking lot and want to fight him. Or someone would call and threaten the deadbeat's wife or dog, and then it was the deadbeat who showed up at the jail, wanting someone arrested. People had to be really angry to make threats like that.

Rhodes wondered if anyone ever got angry enough to kill.

He closed the notebook and went into the other room. Yancey followed him. Mrs. Burkett wasn't there, but Rhodes could hear her in the kitchen.

He went in there, with Yancey trailing along behind him. Mrs. Burkett was standing beside a sink filled with dirty dishes. On the stove there was an iron skillet about half full of grease. Overton probably cooked his bacon in there every day but poured out the grease about once a month. There were dirty dishes on the little wooden table, too, and on the sink counter. The smell was even worse than in the other rooms. Rhodes didn't think he'd want to eat a meal there.

"I swear, I just don't know where to start," Mrs. Burkett said.

Rhodes didn't have any advice for her. The job seemed almost overwhelming.

He showed her the notebook. "I found this in the office. I'd like to hold onto it if you don't mind."

"Lord, no. Take anything you want. That's one less thing I'll have to deal with. What is it, anyway?"

"Your brother's business records."

"He kept records? Randy?"

"Not very good ones," Rhodes said. "But they might help me. There was something else I wanted to ask you, by the way."

"What?"

"Did your brother know someone named John West?"

"I couldn't say about that. I didn't know many of Randy's friends."

Rhodes was disappointed, but he thought he might as well try the other name.

"What about Pep Yeldell?"

"Oh, Pep. Sure. I knew him all right. He and Randy were buddies."

Rhodes felt the spot between his shoulder blades begin to itch furiously. It was a feeling so real that he wanted to reach around and scratch it, but he restrained himself.

"Pep and Randy used to run around together all the time," Mrs. Burkett said. Then she stopped talking and looked surprised, as if something had just occurred to her. "That's funny."

"What's funny?" Rhodes asked.

"Not funny. Peculiar. You know what I mean."

Rhodes said that he knew the feeling but not what she meant about something being funny.

"You know. Pep dying the way he did, and now Randy. I tried to get Randy to stop smoking all the time, but it didn't do any good. And it would never have done any good to tell either one of them to stop drinking." She shook her head. "And just look where it got them."

"I'm sorry," Rhodes said.

"Thank you." Mrs. Burkett looked at the notebook that Rhodes was holding. "I don't guess Randy mentioned anything about money. Do you think he had any?"

"I don't know," Rhodes said, looking around the kitchen. "There's not any mention of a bank account in here. But he might have had some money."

Mrs. Burkett smiled ruefully. "I know what you're thinking. If he had anything at all, he sure didn't spend it around here. All he did was leave me with a mess to clean up."

She looked down at Yancey, who was sniffing at something on the floor. Rhodes wasn't sure what it was. It looked a little like a stick, but it might have been a piece of nearly petrified bacon.

"Well, I guess he left me with more than a mess," Mrs. Burkett said. "He left me his dog, too. And then there's that old car out there in the driveway. It hasn't been driven in twenty years. Maybe more than that. Lord knows what I'm going to do with it."

"Now there's something I might be able to help you with," Rhodes said.

TWENTY

RHODES DROVE HOME with no idea how he was going to explain to Ivy that they were the proud owners of both a 1958 Edsel and a Pomeranian named Yancey.

He didn't know how he was going to explain it to Speedo, either, not that Speedo would mind the car part. It was the new dog part that he might not understand.

Rhodes still wasn't quite sure just exactly how he'd gotten Yancey as part of the deal. It just seemed that by the time he and Mrs. Burkett had finished talking about the Edsel, he had agreed to take the dog to boot.

He was too soft-hearted when it came to animals, that was it. In fact, he'd gotten Speedo pretty much the same way, while he was working on an earlier investigation.

Yancey was with him now in the front seat of the county car, sitting on the remains of the yellow towel and looking more like a dust mop than ever. He was too small to put his feet on the window and look out, though he'd tried to do so a couple of times. He'd given up soon enough, and now he was just sitting there, breathing, the pink tip of his tongue sticking out of his mouth.

Another little problem that Rhodes was going to

have to deal with was the fact that Yancey wasn't exactly the rugged, outdoors type. He was used to the comfortable environment found inside a house, if you could call the environment in Overton's house comfortable. Whatever it had been, it was better than the weather outside the car. The temperature had dropped below freezing, and it would no doubt continue to drop all through the night.

The good news was that Yancey was housebroken. There was plenty of evidence of human uncleanliness in Overton's house, and thank goodness Rhodes hadn't looked in the bathroom, but there was no evidence of canine uncleanliness.

"All you have to do is take him outside for a while in the morning and in the late afternoon," Mrs. Burkett had told Rhodes. "That's what Randy always did."

Rhodes didn't really believe it. Overton might have opened the door and let the dog out and opened it again to let him back in, but he wasn't the type to take him out and walk with him. Yancey didn't even have a collar, much less a leash.

Rhodes tried to think of how to break the news to Ivy. He didn't know whether to bring up the car first, or the dog. The car was going to be a little touchy, since it involved money.

Yancey had come as a bonus, but he'd had to give Mrs. Burkett a check for the car. It wasn't much. She hadn't asked for much, and Rhodes had no idea what the car was worth. He just knew that he wanted it, so he didn't try to bargain. He gave her what she asked.

But Rhodes knew the check was just the beginning. There was body work to be done, and then there would have to be a new paint job. Rhodes hadn't even looked at the interior, but the seats couldn't be in very good shape, not unless they'd been reupholstered sometime in the last forty years. And there was bound to be some engine repair needed. For all Rhodes knew, birds were nesting under the hood. It was all going to run into a lot more money, he was sure.

When Rhodes arrived at his house, it was nearly 6:30. Ivy was already there. The lights in the living room and the kitchen were on.

Rhodes drove into the driveway and stopped the car. "Well, Yancey, this is it. What do you think?"

Yancey didn't move, though it was barely possible that the pace of his breathing increased a bit.

"You're not a lot of help," Rhodes said. "I guess I'm going to have to do this on my own."

He grabbed Yancey, got out of the car, and walked to the front porch. Instead of going inside, he rang the bell. When Ivy opened the door, Rhodes held up Yancey and said, "I brought you a present."

YANCEY TOOK to his new home right away. Rhodes put the remnants of the towel in a corner of the utility room near the washer and dryer, and Yancey lay down on it and promptly went to sleep. Ivy found a couple of plastic tubs that had once held margarine and would do for now to hold Yancey's food and water. She put them on the floor near the blanket.

"He's cute," she said. "Why don't we get him a red collar?"

"Red is fine," Rhodes said.

"Do you think he's had all his shots?"

Considering where Yancey had been living, Rhodes doubted that he had gotten any shots at all. He told Ivy that one of them would have to take Yancey to the vet.

"Which one of us would that be?" she asked.

"Whichever one of us gets the chance. I'm going to be pretty busy for the next few days, though."

"That means me."

"Probably," Rhodes said. "And after all, he's your dog."

"Ah. I'd almost forgotten that. A present, you said."

"That's right."

"Besides the present, what else did you find at the late Mr. Overton's house?"

Rhodes had already told her about Overton's "accident." Now he told her about Overton's notebook and how it might actually be a clue, thanks to Overton's record-keeping.

"Overton and Pep Yeldell were good friends," he said. "And several of the people that Overton worked for had good reason to dislike both him and Yeldell. Grat Bilson and Bull Lowery for two. And there were a couple of other names in there. Mack Riley and Ty Berry. Berry seems to know an awful lot about Yeldell for some reason. And Mack Riley's tied in with both Bilson and Berry, so I might as well talk to him, too."

"Tonight?"

Rhodes didn't want to go out again, but he said, "Well, I can get started."

"Who's going to tell Speedo about his new brother?"

"I thought I'd let you do that. Yancey's your dog, after all."

"I thought you might say that. What if Speedo's jealous that Yancey gets to sleep inside?"

"Remind him that he has his own private residence. Well insulated, too. Styrofoam walls, straw on the floor. What more could he ask for?"

"Right."

"You don't sound convinced. You'd better practice before you talk to him."

"Right. And what about supper?"

"Haven't you fed him yet?"

"Of course I fed him," Ivy said. "I was talking about *your* supper."

"What are my choices?"

"Meatloaf, with scalloped potatoes. Do you have time?"

"I'll make time," Rhodes told her. "There's something else we have to talk about."

TWENTY-ONE

AFTER HE'D EATEN, Rhodes drove by the jail to check in and see what was going on.

"It's Saturday night," Hack said. "You want to hear any more?"

"It's not generally as bad as Friday," Rhodes said.

Friday was payday for a lot of people, many of whom seemed unable to wait until Saturday to spend their money on wine, women, and honky-tonk music.

"It's pretty quiet, to tell the truth," Lawton said. He was standing near the door that led to the cells. "Buddy hasn't had to bring anybody in yet except one kid."

Hack turned to Lawton. "I'm the one he asked about what was goin' on. It's for me to say how quiet it is."

"Okay, okay, I was just tryin' to help out. You gonna tell him about the kid or not?"

"He's not a kid," Hack said.

Lawton disagreed. "Looks like a kid to me."

"That's because you're older'n dirt your ownself. Ever'body under a hundred looks like a kid to you."

Lawton grinned. "I wouldn't say that. *You* don't look like a kid. And then there's Miz McGee."

Hack stood up. "You better not say nothin' about Miz McGee."

Rhodes thought for a second that he might, just this once, stand back and see what would happen if he didn't intervene. Probably nothing at all. Hack and Lawton would jaw at one another for a few minutes and then forget all about their differences. He should just let them go.

But he couldn't do it. He said, "Let's don't get off the subject here. What about the kid?"

"He ain't no kid," Hack said, sitting down and turning his back on Lawton.

"What about the prisoner, then?" Rhodes said.

Lawton turned the knob of the door and opened it slightly. He was clearly planning to make a break for it.

"He's just a kid," Lawton said before plunging through the door and closing it behind him.

Hack picked up a stapler as if he were going to throw it, but of course he didn't. He put it back down on the desk and said, "He's twenty-two. That ain't no kid."

"I'm willing to concede the point," Rhodes said. "But only if you'll tell me the whole story."

"He hit somebody," Hack said.

Rhodes waited.

So did Hack.

"Why?" Rhodes asked after a full minute had passed.

"It was over a toothpick," Hack said.

In his career in law enforcement, Rhodes had

heard a lot of reasons for fights. A toothpick had never been among them, however.

"You're telling me he got into a fight with somebody over a toothpick?"

"You might say that."

"I don't want to know about what I *might* say. Tell me what happened."

Hack settled back in his chair. "They were at that new cafe that opened up out on the highway, Ruby Lee's. You been there yet?"

"Not yet. I haven't had a chance. Just tell me about the fight."

"Well, these two fellas weren't together, but they paid out one after another at the register. Johnny Banks, that's the prisoner, was in line behind the other one. His name's Elbert Haskins. You know either one of 'em?"

Rhodes said that he didn't.

"I know Haskins a little," Hack said. "He's a big bingo player out at the VFW on Tuesday nights."

"I'm sure he is, but we can talk about that some other time. What happened at the cafe?"

"Haskins got him a toothpick at the register. They got this little antique toothpick holder there that looks like a woodpecker standin' by a log. The log's full of toothpicks, and if you push the woodpecker's head down, he picks one up in his bill."

"All right. Haskins got a toothpick. Then what?"

"Banks asked him not to use it. Said it was impolite to pick your teeth in a public place. Said his grandma taught him better when he was just a kid."

Hack paused and turned to look at the door through which Lawton had disappeared. "He ain't no kid now, though."

"I got that part," Rhodes said. "Tell me what happened next."

"Well, they got to arguin'. Then they got to shovin'. Then the hittin' started and somebody called us."

"Assault," Rhodes said, glad that they were nearly to the end of the story. "Banks was arrested for assault."

"And batt'ry."

"What about Haskins?"

"He's at the hospital. Buddy thinks he's got a broken rib or two. That Banks kid's pretty good-sized."

Rhodes just sat there, smiling and not saying a word.

It took a few seconds for Hack to catch on. Then he said, "I didn't mean he was a kid. What I meant was—"

"Never mind," Rhodes said. "It's not important."

"You ain't gonna say anything to Lawton are you?"

"Not a word. Trust me."

"I've heard that one before," Hack said.

"You don't have to worry about me. I can keep a secret. What else do you have to tell me about the kid? I mean the prisoner?"

"He called his grandma. Says she'll be right down to bail him out. Says she's proud of him for bustin' Haskins. She'd have done the same in his place, he says."

"I'm sorry I won't be here to meet her," Rhodes said.

"I bet you are," Hack said.

ACTUALLY RHODES FELT lucky not to have a few broken ribs himself. Ivy had taken the news about the car much better than he'd thought she would.

"How much?" she'd asked.

Rhodes had told her. "But that won't be the end of it. There's sure to be more expense."

"A four-door hardtop, you said?"

"Right. Red and white."

"They don't make four-door hardtops anymore, do they?"

"No," Rhodes said. "The roof of a hardtop doesn't have a lot of support. You wouldn't want to have a wreck in one, especially not if it rolled."

"I wouldn't want to have a wreck in anything."

"We won't be having any wrecks. We'll just drive it in town."

"Like the little old maid. Never take it out of the garage except to go to church."

"Something like that," Rhodes said.

"What about insurance?"

That was something Rhodes hadn't thought about. "I'll leave that to you. You work at the agency, after all."

"I'll check on it tomorrow. Can't you get some kind of special license plates for antique cars?"

Rhodes hadn't thought of that, either. It was hard

for him to think of something as an antique if it wasn't even as old as he was. But he knew Ivy was right. They could get the special plates.

"People will want us to drive it in parades," Ivy said. "Maybe we can be part of the celebration at the Old Settlers' Grounds."

"Maybe."

"That reminds me of something," Ivy said. "I was thinking about Pep Yeldell today."

"What did you think?"

"Well, you know it's pretty absurd to think that someone could murder a person by suggesting that he go swimming at the Old Settlers' Grounds. Even if you could find someone to make the suggestion, you couldn't be sure he'd do it. And if he did, how could you count on him swinging on the rope? He might, but then he might not. It just doesn't make sense."

"I know," Rhodes said. "You're right. Maybe it was just an accident after all. That's what Dr. White thought. But I know someone killed Overton. I'm sure of it. And Overton was Yeldell's good buddy. Yeldell knew West. It might all tie together."

"I wasn't saying what you seem to think I did," Ivy told him.

"You'd better make it simple enough so that I can get it, then," Rhodes said. "All these accidents have got me confused."

"I'm saying that limb didn't have to fall out of the tree and hit him."

"Why not?"

"Wouldn't you get pretty much the same effect

if you hit him in the head with the limb yourself?'' Ivy asked.

Rhodes just sat there for a while, feeling stupid. Then he said, ''Sure you would.''

TWENTY-TWO

RHODES THOUGHT he might as well begin with Ty Berry, who didn't have any known ties to either John West or Pep Yeldell but who had certainly been associated with Randall Overton.

Berry lived not too far from the jail on one of the older residential streets in town. It was a lot like the street Rhodes lived on—big pecan trees, cracked sidewalks, and cars parked on the street. Berry wasn't happy to see Rhodes, but he invited him in.

"I hope you're not here campaigning to get my vote," he said.

The living room wasn't at all what Rhodes had expected. Berry was a bachelor, but he didn't live like Randall Overton. There wasn't a speck of dust anywhere, the hardwood floors gleamed, the couch was draped with an afghan, and woven throws hung over the backs of the two comfortable-looking chairs. There were real oil paintings on the wall, and they didn't even have bluebonnets in them. Rhodes was pretty sure that the china doll in one of the chairs was a genuine antique, much older than his Edsel.

"I'd ask you to sit down," Berry said, "but I don't think you'll be staying long."

"That depends," Rhodes said.

"On what?"

"On your answers to a few questions."

"What questions?"

"We'll start with a few about Randall Overton."

"Oh," Berry said. "Him. Maybe you'd better sit down after all."

BERRY HAD HIRED Overton for the remodeling job because Overton had come by and offered to fix Berry's roof.

"He said he could fix up the roof like new for five hundred," Berry said. "I had a couple of leaks, and I'd been thinking about a new roof, which would have cost several thousand. Overton's offer seemed like a good way to save some money and stop the leaks at the same time."

"Did it work out?"

"Well, we never really got around to the roof. I'd been thinking about having my kitchen redone, too, so while we were talking, I asked if he'd ever done any remodeling work. He said he was an expert, that he'd done lots of remodeling. He even gave me the names of some references."

"But you didn't call them," Rhodes said.

Berry nodded. "But I didn't call them. I thought that he wouldn't have given the names if he'd been worried about me calling. So I didn't bother."

"Big mistake."

"No kidding. But I didn't much like the people whose names he gave, and I thought it wouldn't matter anyway. It did matter, of course."

"Whose names did he give?"

"Grat Bilson was one."

"Well, I can see why you didn't want to call him."

"We got along a little better in those days," Berry said. "I sure wish I'd called him."

"How much did Overton get from you?"

"Quite a bit. He needed to buy the materials, he said, so I gave him the money for that in advance."

"Big mistake number two," Rhodes said.

"Absolutely. I knew better, but I gave him the money anyway. It was a lot of money, because I wanted nice cabinets. Overton came back, tore out my cabinets and got started on the job. He seemed to be having a little trouble, and he started skipping days. Then he skipped a week or so, came back once, and after that I hardly ever saw him again."

"What do you mean by 'hardly ever'?"

Berry looked pained. "He came by now and then to promise he'd get the work done within the week. Two weeks would go by, and he'd show up again, do a little hammering and leave."

"How long did that go on?"

"Months. Nearly a year. After that I just kissed my money good-bye and hired someone else to do the job."

"Did you check his references?"

"It's not funny, Sheriff."

"I wasn't laughing," Rhodes said. "Just how angry were you about all this?"

"I heard about Overton," Berry said. "What he did to me happened more than two years ago, and I've pretty much gotten over it. I'd certainly never kill anyone because of something like that."

"You weren't exactly shy about waving that shotgun around last night."

"That was a different situation. Besides, the shotgun wasn't loaded."

Rhodes didn't know whether to believe that or not. He said, "Did you ever have any dealings with John West?"

"What's he got to do with this?"

"Maybe nothing. Did you know him?"

"I know he got run over. Are you trying to blame me for that?"

Rhodes said, "I just wondered if you knew him."

"I bought a battery from him once. Got a good deal, and the battery lasted longer than the guarantee. Is that what you mean?"

Rhodes wasn't sure what he meant. He was just following his usual method of asking questions and trying to catch somebody in a contradiction or a lie. Maybe a computer could do it better.

"And Pep Yeldell?" he asked. "What about him?"

"I never saw him before that morning that I called you. Why? Do you think I killed him, too?"

"I don't think you killed anybody. I'm just trying to get a few things straight in my mind."

"Well, you're looking in the wrong place. You ought to be talking to Faye Knape. I still think she's in on it. Or talk to Grat Bilson. If Overton wasn't lying, he did some work for Grat, and Grat sure didn't like Yeldell. If I were the sheriff, he's the one I'd suspect."

Berry's tone didn't leave any doubt about what

he thought of Rhodes's intellectual and investigative abilities. Rhodes didn't mind. He'd already lost Berry's vote.

"Can you tell me where you were the night Yeldell died?" he asked.

"I don't remember, but I can tell you where I was last night. I was at a called meeting of the Sons and Daughters. We talked about how we were going to counter the protests that are being planned against the Native American dances at our celebration. There are plenty of witnesses."

There hadn't been a time of death established for Randall Overton, but Rhodes didn't bother to tell Berry that. Maybe Berry was in the clear, or maybe not. He'd have to talk to Dr. White and get an estimate.

"You might be thinking about where you were on the night Yeldell died, just in case," Rhodes said.

Berry's face was red, and Rhodes wondered if he might be thinking about going for his shotgun. It was probably as good a time as any to change the subject, so he asked if Faye Knape had been by to see Berry and to talk to him about cooperating on the celebration. As it turned out, she had.

"But she's the one who's not going to cooperate, I can tell you that," Berry said.

"Cooperation is a two-way street," Rhodes told him. "It even involves compromise now and then."

"It was the Sons and Daughters who came up with the idea of the celebration. We ought to be the ones who run it."

"You could use some help. Everyone needs help now and then."

Berry half smiled. "Are you implying that you helped me out by talking to the Burleson heirs?"

"Nope," Rhodes said. "I wasn't even going to mention it."

"You won't have to. Faye Knape did. I think you've lost her vote, too."

"Before this is all over, I won't have any votes at all. But I didn't come here to get your vote. Tell me about some of Overton's other references."

"I don't know that I want to, now that I know what you're after. I'm not going to send you out to harass any of my friends."

"I've already got a list of names," Rhodes said. "I'll be talking to them anyway."

"I can't remember any other names," Berry said. "Except for Mack Riley."

"What about Mack and John West? Did they know each other? Did Mack know Pep Yeldell?"

Berry's mouth tightened. Then he said, "I may as well tell you. You'll find out about it anyway."

Maybe Berry didn't think Rhodes was such a bad investigator, after all.

"I'm sure I would," Rhodes said. "So go ahead and tell me."

"Mack had a little run-in with Yeldell one time. Now, I never met Yeldell, but I told you the other morning that I'd heard of him. Mack was really upset by something Yeldell had done to his car. He said Yeldell ought to be horsewhipped or worse."

"When did he say that?"

"It was after a meeting of the Sons and Daughters one time. The one in September, I think. Mack had come just to listen, but he was talking to someone after it was over, and they must have gotten into a discussion of cars. I didn't hear the whole thing, and I don't know who he was talking to, but a lot of people heard him."

"I guess I'd better have a talk with Mack, then," Rhodes said.

"That's what I'd do," Berry told him. "If I were the sheriff."

TWENTY-THREE

MACK RILEY lived in one of the oldest houses in Clearview, a big two-story wood home that had been built in the early years of the century.

Rhodes had been impressed by the place in his boyhood. In those days it had been out at the edge of town, and it had been the first thing you could see from the highway when you were coming in from the north. Now it was practically surrounded by some of the newer additions to Clearview's economy: a video store, the McDonald's, and a convenience store that sold food, gasoline, and lottery tickets.

Mack wasn't much in the way of a yard man; there were bare patches of ground, and weeds dotted the dead grass that remained. A wide porch extended around three-quarters of the house, and an old wooden swing dangled from the porch ceiling near the front door. Several of its slats were rotted nearly in half, and Rhodes wondered when someone had last sat in it.

Rhodes opened the screen and knocked on the door, the upper half of which held a big piece of beveled glass. A thin curtain hung over the glass on the inside, and through it Rhodes could see a dark shape moving down the hall toward the door.

Mack Riley opened the door, but not all the way.

He wasn't any happier to see Rhodes than Berry had been. Mack was wearing a ragged old maroon chenille bathrobe that hung about to the middle of his skinny calves and worn-out house shoes that looked as if they'd seen their best days sometime around 1955.

"If it's about that little set-to that I had with Grat Bilson," he said, "I'm sorry about it, but he was downright insulting to me. I couldn't just let it go."

The wind was whipping at Rhodes's jacket, and the boards in the old porch were creaking in the cold.

"It's not about Bilson," Rhodes said. "If I could come in for a minute, I'd like to ask you a few things about Randall Overton."

"He's worse than Grat Bilson," Mack said. "He's nothing but a common thief, no matter what he calls himself."

"He's not anything anymore," Rhodes said. "He's dead. That's what I want to talk to you about."

Mack opened the door wide enough for Rhodes to enter. It was just as cold in the hallway as it had been outside.

"Who killed Overton?" Mack asked, closing the door.

Rhodes rubbed his hands together. "I didn't say anybody killed him."

Mack walked past Rhodes and down the hall. There was a stairway leading up on the right and a bookcase on the left. Rhodes nearly had to turn sideways to get between them.

"You might as well come on in the parlor," Mack said. "It's the only warm room in the house."

He opened a door on the left and Rhodes followed him into a room that had a small fireplace. Instead of being filled with burning wood, the fireplace held a gas heater that was going full blast. The room was almost stuffy after the hallway, and there was condensation on the window pane. There wasn't much furniture. There were two wooden rocking chairs with cushions in the seats, a floral couch, and a scarred coffee table sitting on a throw rug. A light fixture holding three naked bulbs dangled from the ceiling on a flaking gilt chain. There was a gun cabinet in one corner. There were at least a couple of weapons in it. Rhodes could see a shotgun and a rifle that looked like a .30-.30.

"This chair's mine," Mack said, taking the one nearer the fire. "You can sit in the other one. Then you can tell me who killed Overton."

The floor creaked when Rhodes sat in the chair.

"I didn't say he was killed," he told Mack.

"Well, he should have been. How did he die, then?"

"He burned to death in his car sometime last night or early this morning. It might have been an accident, or it might not."

Mack glanced down at a thick paperback book lying on the floor beside his chair.

Rhodes noticed the glance and said, "What are you reading?"

"Charles Dickens. I don't own a TV set. Wouldn't have one of them in the house. So I read a lot. You get you a book by Dickens, you've got plenty of good reading.''

Rhodes had read a book by Dickens once when he was in junior high school. He'd even given a book report on it. *David Copperfield*. It had taken him a long time to get to the end of it.

"I always liked Charles Dickens," he said.

Mack looked surprised. "You read Dickens?"

"*David Copperfield*. It was sort of based on Dickens's life."

Rhodes hoped he was remembering that part right. It had been a long time since that book report. Since about the time the Edsel was new, most likely.

Mack rocked forward and picked up the book by his chair. He rocked back and held up the book so Rhodes could see the cover.

"This is *Bleak House*," Mack said. "It's a mystery in a way. You might like it. There's a man who dies by spontaneous combustion."

Rhodes wondered if Hack had read the book. And then he wondered if Mack Riley might have gotten the idea for killing Overton from it.

"Things like that happen," Mack said. "Spontaneous combustion, I mean. The policeman in this book's named Bucket, by the way. Inspector Bucket."

Rhodes didn't want to get into a literary discussion. "I understand that you knew Pep Yeldell."

"Another common thief. Not on quite the same scale as Overton, but a thief nevertheless."

"So you knew him?"

"Know him? I threatened to horsewhip him. As

I'm sure you know. Otherwise you'd be discussing Charles Dickens with someone else tonight.''

Rhodes didn't think there was much chance of that. He would have bet that Mack was the only person in Clearview who'd read Dickens in years. Unless they still required book reports in junior high school these days. Rhodes wasn't sure about that.

"How much did he take you for?" Rhodes asked.

"Yeldell? Or Overton?"

"You can start with Yeldell."

"I know what you think." Mack dropped the book to the floor. It struck with a solid thump. "You think I'm an old fool, and I guess I am. I got taken not once but twice. But the first time was different."

"How?"

"I let Yeldell do some work on a car of mine. He did body work for Bull Lowery, but he was a shade-tree mechanic, too. He'd put on a muffler for me once, and he changed my plugs a time or two. He did just fine both times, so I let him do a brake job. He said he'd put on new pads and get the rotors turned, and he'd do it all for about half what a regular mechanic would charge."

"But it didn't work out?"

"The brakes were worse after he worked on them than they were before. I took the car back two or three times, but he could never seem to get them fixed. They squealed like a cat was under the car somewhere. I finally took it in to the Ford place, and they told me that the pads were worn out and the rotors needed turning. Yeldell hadn't done a damn thing to it. He charged me for parts and work that he never did.''

No wonder Yeldell and Overton had been such good buddies, Rhodes thought. They had developed a similar approach to business entrepreneurship. He wondered who had learned from whom.

''You can see why I said what I did,'' Mack said. ''I was just trying to warn other people away from Yeldell. No need for somebody else to get cheated.''

''And Overton? What did he do?''

''He suckered me in on a paint job. Came by looking at roofs in the neighborhood, but mine's in pretty good shape, and I told him so. He looked around inside a little and said he noticed that the walls were pretty bad, and they were. Used to have wallpaper on them, but that all came down long ago. I had the walls Sheetrocked and painted then, but the paint was dirty and faded by the time Overton saw it. So I asked how much he'd charge to paint them. He gave me a good price.''

''And you paid him in advance,'' Rhodes said.

Mack rocked back and forth a few times. ''Fool that I was, I did. And if anybody should have known better, it's me. I've dealt with painters and Mr. Fix-its for a long time, but he was the first one that ever took me. He never painted but two rooms, and those looked like they'd been done by a horse dipping its tail in a paint can and slinging it around. I was out nearly a thousand dollars, and I had to have it all done again.''

''But you didn't threaten to horsewhip Overton.''

''The hell I didn't. It's just that nobody heard me.

I went over to his house and told him right to his big flat face what I thought of him. Didn't do a damn bit of good, though.''

''You could have reported him.''

''And what would have happened? He'd pay a twenty-five dollar fine or sit in jail a day or two. I still wouldn't have my money back.''

Rhodes looked at the window. There wasn't much to see outside. It was too dark. But he could hear the wind sighing around the house.

''I didn't kill either one of them,'' Mack said. He spread his hands, looked at the palms, and clasped them together. ''I admit I was mad enough to do it at the time, but I didn't. I never killed anybody in my life, except in Korea in the war, and I'm not even sure about that. I was just shooting in the dark, mostly.''

''And I guess you didn't know John West, either.''

''What's he got to do with this?''

''He knew Yeldell. Yeldell and Overton were best friends.''

''You've got three men dead by accident, don't you?'' Mack said. ''That sounds like a lot, all right, but I didn't kill 'em.''

''Maybe not. Where were you the night West died?''

''When was that?''

Rhodes told him.

''Then I was sitting right here in this room. I was reading *Our Mutual Friend* about that time. There's a drowning in that one, if you're thinking I've been getting ideas from books.''

"I don't think that," Rhodes said, but along with the spontaneous combustion, it was enough to make a man wonder.

ALTHOUGH RHODES TALKED to Riley for several more minutes, he got no more information from him. In fact, the longer they talked, the more stubborn Riley became, and Rhodes got the distinct impression that Riley wasn't telling all he knew.

But that was to be expected. If you were the sheriff, people lied to you now and then. Rhodes was used to it. He didn't like it, but he knew that he usually found out the truth sooner or later.

He told Riley that he had to be going, and Riley had no objections.

"You're barking up the wrong tree talking to me," Riley said as he showed Rhodes to the door. "I'd help you if I could, but I just don't know a thing."

Once more, Rhodes got the feeling that he was being lied to, but he forgot about it when he got to the car and Hack came on the radio, telling him that he'd better get himself out to The County Line.

"I think maybe there's a riot goin' on," Hack said.

TWENTY-FOUR

"BUDDY'S ALREADY ON the way out there," Hack said. "I tried to get you at home, but Ivy said you were out investigatin'. I'm glad I caught up with you because from what I could tell, Buddy's gonna need some help. You better step on it."

Rhodes said that he would. If someone at The County Line had actually called in a disturbance, there was bound to be big trouble. The owners of the honky-tonk didn't like having outsiders settling any little squabbles that happened to arise in their establishment. In most cases, they preferred to let the participants settle things themselves and then send the losers to the emergency room. Sometimes the winners had to go, too. But now and then things got completely out of hand and someone called the law. This looked to be one of those times.

So Rhodes hurried. He even turned on the siren.

WHEN HE GOT TO The County Line, he could see immediately that things had indeed gotten out of hand. In the glare of the floodlights that illuminated the parking lot, little knots of men and women were pushing and shoving and slugging one another with fists and the occasional longneck beer bottle.

They were rolling in the white rock chips that topped the parking lot, sprawling across car hoods, and flailing around in pickup beds. The siren and the strobing light bar didn't bother them at all. Rhodes was pretty sure that no one ever noticed them. It would be hard to hear with the wind and all the shouting that was undoubtedly going on. It was one of the biggest fights Rhodes had ever seen.

And Rhodes knew that it was just the spillover. Whatever was going on inside the building was bound to be worse.

He parked the car and got out. The north wind whipped the dust off the parking lot and drove it against his pants legs, along with the greasy wrapper from somebody's hamburger. He shut his eyes for a second while he reached down to pull the paper off his leg. Then he walked forward, shoving his way through a tight clump of men who were butting each other in the forehead and screaming creative obscenities.

Rhodes pulled at them, trying to separate them, but it was no use. He might as well have been invisible for all the attention they paid him. He thought about getting his shotgun out of the car and firing off a few rounds to get their attention, but he decided that he'd better go inside first. Buddy must be in there somewhere. His county car was parked not far from where Rhodes had parked his own.

Rhodes had been in one near-riot at The County Line recently, but it paled in comparison to the one he walked into. There were more people, for one thing, and they were considerably more energetic. It looked like a climactic fight scene from one of John

Wayne's later movies, *North to Alaska* maybe, or *McLintock!*

The band at the back of the dance floor was still playing, safe for the time being behind its chicken-wire screen. Rhodes couldn't hear the tune, whatever it was. The fighting was too noisy.

Women were fighting women, women were fighting men, men were fighting men, and Buddy was standing on the bar, his mouth moving and the tendons on his neck standing out. Rhodes couldn't hear him any more than the brawlers could.

The bartender, a very large man named Zach, was standing under a neon Coors sign, his arms crossed and a look of sad resignation on his face.

A beer bottle flew toward Rhodes's head. He moved quickly to one side, and the bottle shattered on the door frame. That did it. He turned and went back outside. For just the fraction of a second he thought about driving his car right through the doorway, siren yowling and lights flashing.

But he wasn't sure the county's insurance would cover the damages, and he was sure the commissioners wouldn't like the idea even a little bit, so he walked on back to the car, shoving aside a couple of men who had locked each other in a mutual unbreakable bear hug. The shove sent them bouncing off a pickup, and they lost their balance, falling to the parking lot. They grunted and groaned, but neither one relinquished his hold.

Rhodes opened the car and got in. He unlocked the shotgun from its stand, checked to see that it was loaded, and got back out.

He didn't want to fire the shotgun outside to begin with. By the time he got everyone's attention, he might be out of shells. He'd save that for later.

He walked to the open door of The County Line, avoiding a threesome of free-swinging cowboys who tumbled out just as he got there, and stepped inside.

Buddy was still up on the bar, but this time so was someone else Rhodes recognized.

Yvonne Bilson. She was struggling to get her foot out of the grasp of someone who was trying to drag her back into the fray. Rhodes couldn't see who it was.

Zach caught sight of Rhodes and the shotgun about then, and Rhodes saw the bartender's eyes widen.

Rhodes smiled and aimed the gun at the ceiling. He looked up just to make sure there was no one hanging from the rafters. There wasn't, so he pulled the trigger.

The noise wasn't deafening—The County Line was too spacious for that. But the boom echoed off the walls and got the attention of the less energetic fighters.

It got Buddy's attention, too. He increased the volume of his yelling, and Rhodes could almost hear him. He fired off another round, and as flakes of plywood drifted down from above, the fighting slacked off considerably.

Rhodes could hear the faint sound of the siren from outside, and he could also hear the band for the first time. The shotgun hadn't discouraged them. They were playing their version of the Faron Young classic "Wine Me Up." It wasn't bad, though Rhodes didn't think it was nearly as good as the original. But then he had always been partial to Faron Young, who was sometimes billed as The Singin' Sheriff.

Rhodes loosed off one more blast, and the fighting pretty much came to a stop. People began getting up off the floor, crawling out from under tables, straightening their clothes, and even shaking hands.

Buddy stopped yelling, hopped down from the bar, and picked his way through the crowd. Rhodes tossed him the shotgun and said, "You go on outside and see if you can calm them down out there. I have to talk to somebody."

Buddy nodded, ejected the empty shell, and went through the door.

Rhodes kept his eyes on Yvonne as he pushed through the mob and over to the bar. She had broken free of whoever had a hand on her, and she was about to slide off the bar and make a run for it.

"Stay right there, Mrs. Bilson," Rhodes called. "I want to talk to you in a minute."

He looked down at the floor, and there was Grat, who was unconscious. Rhodes didn't know who had hit him, but he was willing to put money on Yvonne.

"If your husband comes to, tell him I want to talk to him, too," Rhodes said.

He had been afraid the trouble at The County Line might knock him out of his chance to talk to any of the other people on his list, but there were Grat and Yvonne Bilson almost as if they'd been waiting for him. They hadn't, of course, and Yvonne obviously didn't want to talk to him in the least, but he wasn't going to let her get away. He couldn't tell about Grat, who still wasn't conscious, but he figured Grat wasn't going to want to talk to him, either. It didn't matter. Rhodes was going to talk to him anyway.

First, however, he wanted to talk to Zach and find out how the fight had gotten started.

The bartender remembered Rhodes from his other visits, and to the sheriff's surprise he reached under the bar and brought out a can of Dr Pepper.

"Were you expecting me?" Rhodes asked.

"Nope. I was hoping I'd never see you again, if you want to know the truth. But since you always ask for this stuff, I thought I'd be ready just in case. I don't like for someone to ask for a drink I don't have. Unless it's one of those import beers. I don't mind not having those things. But they make Dr Pepper right here in Texas."

Rhodes reached into his back pocket for his billfold and heard the roar of a shotgun from the parking lot.

"I didn't think he'd have to use it out there," Zach said. "I hope he didn't have to shoot anybody."

"Buddy wouldn't do that," Rhodes said, laying a dollar bill on the bar. "He's a trained lawman."

Zach ignored the bill. "The drink's on the house."

"Take the money," Rhodes told him. "I wouldn't want to be obligated."

Zach took the bill and put it in the cash register. Rhodes popped the can and took a drink. The Dr

Pepper was icy cold, which was the best way to drink it if you had to drink it from a can. Yvonne watched him drink, and Rhodes put down the can to smile at her. She didn't smile back.

Rhodes turned to look at the crowd. Things were getting back to normal. Tables were set upright and one couple was already on the dance floor. The band was playing another old song that Rhodes recognized, "He's in the Jailhouse Now."

"Webb Pierce," Rhodes said.

Zach, who was either too young to remember Webb Pierce or ignorant of his country music heritage or both, said, "Huh?"

"Never mind. What got the fight started?"

Zach nodded toward Yvonne. "She did."

"You son of a bitch," Yvonne said.

Rhodes tried to remember what Ty Berry had said. Something about a limited vocabulary. He had Yvonne pegged, all right.

"What happened?" Rhodes asked Zach.

"Nothing more than usual, at first. She was in here dancin' with some guy when her husband came in. He didn't like it, and he grabbed her. The guy she was dancin' with didn't like *that*, so he slugged her husband. My bouncer got there about that time, and they both slugged *him*. Put him out like a light. I think he's still on the floor out there somewhere."

Rhodes looked back. There was a small group of people standing over someone, trying to pull him to his feet. His knees were rubbery, and he couldn't quite make it. Each time they got him to a standing position, he slid back to the floor.

"That him?" Rhodes asked.

"Yeah," Zach said. "He's been hit before. He'll be all right."

The shotgun boomed outside.

"Buddy must be getting serious with them out there," Rhodes said.

Zach frowned. "I hope he's not sending them home."

"That's what he's doing," Rhodes said, "if I know Buddy. And I do."

"Damn. I hate to lose paying customers."

"They'll be back," Rhodes said.

Zach didn't look convinced. "Maybe. People don't like to be sent home. It's not good for customer relations." He sighed. "Anyway, after those two flattened Roy, the whole place went crazy. But at least no one drove any motorcycles through here this time."

The motorcycle episode was one that Rhodes would just as soon have forgotten about. He took another drink from the Dr Pepper can.

"A few of your customers have had some bad luck since then," he said, setting the can on the bar.

"I heard about them," Zach said. "John West, Pep Yeldell, Randall Overton. They were all good customers. It doesn't do my business any good to lose them. I haven't seen Tuffy in here since he left with his brother that night, and Pep and Randall won't be back for damn sure."

Rhodes wondered if Zach cared about anyone except as a customer. He looked down at the floor where Bilson was sitting up groggily.

"All the ruckus you stirred up out here that time didn't help much, either," Zach continued. "And we didn't even go to the state play-off."

Rhodes was suddenly tired of talking to Zach. He said, "I don't think I'll need to make any arrests out here tonight, but I'd like to talk to the Bilsons somewhere in private if you have somewhere I could use."

"You can use the office," Zach said, pointing to a door between two pinball machines. "There's nobody in there right now."

"That'll do," Rhodes said. "I have to go out and check on Buddy first. You make sure the Bilsons don't try to leave."

Zach wasn't enthusiastic about that idea. "I'm not your deputy."

"No, but you could be my prisoner if I got upset with you."

"All right, I get the point. They won't go anywhere."

"You son of a bitch," Yvonne said.

Rhodes was looking forward to having a conversation with her just to test her originality.

"I'll be back in a minute," he told her. "Why don't you see about your husband?"

Yvonne leaned over and looked down at Grat, who was now leaning against the bar, looking dazed. She didn't make any move to help him, however.

"What did you hit him with, anyway?" Rhodes asked.

"Beer bottle," Yvonne said, and she smiled for the first time since Rhodes had entered the building.

TWENTY-FIVE

BUDDY HAD THINGS under control in the parking lot. He'd rounded everyone up and sent them on their separate ways. Cars were pulling out of the lot, and white dust swirled through the light.

"I was just about to win 'em over in there before you showed up," Buddy said.

Rhodes reached for the shotgun. "I could see that. You would have had them on your side in another second or two."

"Less, if I'd carried my shotgun in there with me," Buddy said, handing Rhodes his weapon.

They walked over to the county car, and Rhodes locked the shotgun back in place.

"You want me to stay out here, help you get things sorted out?" Buddy asked.

"I think I've pretty much done that. There are a couple of people I want to question about something else, but I can handle that by myself. You can go back on patrol."

"You don't want to double-team them? Give 'em the old good cop, bad cop?"

"It's Saturday night," Rhodes said. "You'd better get back on the road."

"Right. Thanks for getting out here so fast."

"Johnny on the spot, that's me. That's why I'm a highly paid public servant."

"The county's going broke paying your salary, all right," Buddy said. "Will you be going back by the jail?"

"Not if I can help it," Rhodes told him.

THE COUNTY LINE'S OFFICE was bare and utilitarian. There was a cheap assemble-it-yourself desk that held a computer and monitor. In front of it sat a desk chair, and against one wall there was a couch that sagged in the middle. A mud-colored carpet remnant covered about half the floor. The dark paneled walls were bare, except for a three-year-old Elvira calendar. Over in one corner was Elvira herself, or at least a life-size cutout of her. She was holding a six-pack of Coors.

Yvonne and Grat sat on the couch. Rhodes turned the desk chair backwards and straddled it, facing them.

"Now, then," he said. "Who wants to tell me what's going on here?"

Neither of them said anything. Yvonne yawned and tried to look bored, while Grat still looked a little glassy-eyed.

"I guess it's up to you, Mrs. Bilson," Rhodes said. "Your husband doesn't look quite ready to talk."

Yvonne looked over Rhodes's shoulder at Elvira. "I don't have anything to say."

"She'uz runnin' 'round on me 'gin," Bilson said.

His voice was weak and his speech was slurred, but Rhodes could hear him all right. So could Yvonne, who didn't like what he said at all.

"I was running around on him again because he killed Pep," she said. "That's why."

That was the most interesting thing that Rhodes had ever heard Yvonne say.

"Why don't you tell me about that," he said.

Grat didn't think that was a good idea. "Don't listen to 'er. She's lyin'."

"You son of a bitch," Yvonne said, reverting to her favorite phrase. "You're the one who told me."

"I think I gotta 'cussion," Bilson said. "Need to go to the 'mergency room."

Rhodes thought Bilson might have a point, but he wasn't ready for a trip to the hospital, not while Yvonne was being so forthcoming.

"I'll take you when your wife tells me her story," he said. "The sooner she gets it told, the sooner we'll go to the emergency room."

Yvonne looked at Rhodes, and then she looked at her husband. She didn't appear to think very much of either one of them.

"You don't have a cigarette, do you?" she asked Rhodes.

"I don't smoke. Are you going to tell me about Pep or not?"

"What the hell," Yvonne said. "Grat killed Pep because he was jealous of him."

"How do you know that?" Rhodes asked.

"Grat said so. It was just after we found out that Randy Overton was dead. He said he was glad of it, and he was glad Pep was dead too. They were two of a kind, he said, and the world was better off without them."

"Didn' kill 'em, though," Bilson said.

"Yes, he did. Randy was with me and Pep that night John West—"

Bilson flopped around on the couch and tried to hit her, but he wasn't successful. He fell across her lap and lay there with his eyes closed, breathing quietly. Yvonne didn't try to move him.

"Like I was saying," she went on, resting one hand on the back of Grat's head, "Randy was Pep's friend, and he was with us the night John West got killed. That's the last time me and Pep went out together. Grat came after me that time, too."

"When I asked you before, you said you didn't remember the last time you saw Pep."

"Well, I did. But I didn't want to talk about it."

"We won't worry about that for a while, then. Let me see if I've got this straight. You'd told Grat that you weren't going with Pep anymore, but you were. Grat found out and killed Pep."

"That's right," Yvonne said. "He's always been the jealous type."

"But why did he kill Randy?"

"He didn't like Randy because he got to us on a remodeling deal, but I bet he killed him because he knew about Grat killing Pep."

Grat pushed himself up slowly and moved back to his side of the couch.

"I didn't kill anybody," he said. His short nap had done him good. His eyes were clear and so was his speech. "And I never said that I did. She just used that as an excuse to come dancing."

"What did you say, exactly?" Rhodes asked.

"Just what she said I did, that Yeldell and Overton were two of a kind and the world was better off without them. It's the truth, isn't it? They were both cheats and liars. Yeldell was worse than that though. He's the one that tried to steal my wife."

Rhodes wanted to get back to another topic, one that really intrigued him.

"What happened when you came after Yvonne the night John West died?"

"Not a thing. There wasn't even a fight that time. I found him and Yvonne and took her home."

"Pep would've fought you," Yvonne said. "But he and Randy had other things on their minds."

"Sure," Bilson said. "Finding somebody else to screw out of a few hundred dollars. Or finding a couple of women to dance with."

"You're just saying that because you're jealous and a killer."

This time Bilson didn't swing at her. He just sighed and said, "I didn't kill anybody. I took you home and put you to bed. Then I watched TV for a while and thought about what I ought to do. I didn't do it, though."

"Yes, you did. You killed him!"

"That wasn't what I was thinking about. I was thinking about a divorce."

"A divorce?" Yvonne was shocked. "Why would you want a divorce?"

Rhodes thought he'd better interrupt before Grat tried to answer that one.

"What about last night?" he asked. "Where were you then?"

"I was at home," Bilson said. "I'm always at home."

"You couldn't prove it by me," Yvonne said. "I was at my sister's."

Bilson sighed. "That's what she always says. She wasn't at her sister's. You can ask her sister if you don't believe me. She was here."

"You son of a bitch," Yvonne said.

Rhodes was going to ask her to come up with a new expression, but then he thought of something.

"Why is it that you remember being with Pep on the night John West was killed?"

"I thought you knew that," Yvonne said. "John was with us, too."

TWENTY-SIX

RHODES FELT A surge of anger. He hadn't known that at all, mainly because no one had told him. Zach, his only semireliable witness, at The County Line hadn't been able to remember a thing. But Yvonne remembered. Rhodes had seen something in her eyes when he'd mentioned West that night at the Burleson cabin, and now he knew what it was.

"Sure," Yvonne said. "We were here at The County Line. We were having a pretty good time until Grat the party pooper showed up."

Rhodes thought about going out for a few words with Zach, but he knew talking to him wouldn't do any good. Maybe Zach really *didn't* remember who had been with John West on that night.

West, Yeldell, and Overton, all in the same place at the same time. And Yvonne Bilson was there too.

Not to mention Grat.

"You told me you'd never met West," he said.

"We weren't introduced," Grat said. "It wasn't exactly a formal social situation. I didn't know who was sitting at the table except for Yvonne and Yeldell. I wasn't paying much attention to anyone else."

"What do you remember about that evening?" Rhodes asked Yvonne.

She glared at her husband. "I remember I was having a good time until *he* got here."

"I was thinking more about John West. Did he seem worried about anything?"

"No. He was having a good time, too. We were all having a good time." She paused. "But anyway, Grat couldn't have met John. John wasn't there when Grat came. He and his brother left early. You know his brother?"

Rhodes was a little disappointed to hear that Grat hadn't met West after all, but he put his disappointment aside for the moment.

"I know Tuffy," he said. "What time did they leave?"

"It was before things really got going good, I know that much. So it was before ten o'clock. Probably closer to nine."

"Was John with anyone?"

"Just Tuffy. He was just drinking and having fun."

Rhodes wondered about that. And he wondered again about who had told Kara West that her husband was seeing other women. But Yvonne wouldn't know about that.

"And you don't know where he was going when he left?" he asked.

"Home, he said. He didn't want his wife to worry about him."

Grat laughed at that. "He didn't want his wife to know where he'd been is more like it."

"I'm sure I didn't ask him," Yvonne said. "It wasn't any of my business."

"Did you see him leave the building?" Rhodes asked.

"No. I was having a good time, too."

"What about Yeldell and Overton? What did they do after your husband came for you?"

"If I was gone, I wouldn't know, would I?"

"I thought you might have some idea. Maybe they mentioned something to you."

"Well, they didn't. I'm sure they stayed right at the table and had some more fun." Her eyes got a faraway look in them. "Pep sure did know how to have a good time."

Rhodes turned his attention to Grat. "Did you go straight home?"

"Where else would I go? I wanted to get somewhere that we could talk in private. Not that we talked. I put her to bed and she went right to sleep. Or maybe she didn't."

Yvonne's look went from faraway to nasty. "What's that supposed to mean?"

"I slept on the couch that night, Sheriff," Grat said. "I can't swear that my wife was in the bedroom all night."

"You son of a bitch," Yvonne said.

Grat ignored her. "It wouldn't be the first time she'd gone out the window. If you're looking for the person who killed John West, maybe it was Yvonne. She could have slipped out the window and driven off in her car, and I never would have known it."

"Was her car damaged the next morning?"

Rhodes asked before Yvonne could express her opinion of Grat yet again.

"I don't know," Grat said. "I didn't look at it. But I do know that it wasn't there when I got home that afternoon."

"Where was it, Mrs. Bilson?" Rhodes asked.

"I took it in to Bull Lowery's body shop for them to look at," Yvonne said. "But not because I hit anybody with it. Why would I want to kill John? I'd just had a little fender bender, and I wanted to get it fixed up."

"Is that right?" Rhodes asked Grat. "About the fender bender?"

"Yeah. She never could drive that car into the garage without hitting the side."

"Did you get the car fixed?"

"No," Yvonne said, looking over his shoulder again. "The estimate was too high. I didn't think it was worth it."

"I'd like to have a look at that car," Rhodes said.

"Sure," Grat said. "Drop by anytime."

Yvonne looked at him and opened her mouth, but this time she didn't have a thing to say.

IN SPITE OF WHAT he'd told Buddy, Rhodes did go back by the jail. Hack was watching a late movie on his little TV set, and Rhodes looked over his shoulder to see what it was.

"*Mansion of the Doomed,*" Hack said. "You ever seen it?"

There had been a time in the not too distant past—before his marriage—that Rhodes had watched more than his share of late movies. Now, it seemed that he generally had other things on his mind.

"Richard Basehart?" he asked.

"If he's the guy that used to be on *Voyage to the Bottom of the Sea,* yeah."

"I've seen it, then."

"You sure? He's out killin' people to get their eyeballs."

"For his blind daughter," Rhodes said. "I've seen it, all right. What's been going on?"

"It's Saturday night."

"Nothing unusual, then?"

"Nothing since that ki—" Hack caught himself. "Since that young fella's grandma came by. She didn't get him out. She thought it might be a good idea if he stayed here overnight."

"She didn't think he should have hit the man who was using the toothpick?"

Hack continued to stare at the TV screen. "She didn't mind that part so much. She thought it might teach the fella a lesson. But she says the front of a cafe isn't the place to teach a lesson like that."

"She's right. Anything else?"

"Just that riot I called you about. I've already heard from Buddy about how he broke it up."

A commercial for a used-car dealer came on. The dealer was dressed in chaps, a huge cowboy hat, and boots. He was riding an elephant and screaming about making the biggest deals in Texas.

"You didn't come by here to tell me about how

Buddy did your job for you, did you?" Hack asked, turning around in his chair.

"No," Rhodes said. "It was something else."

On the drive in from The County Line, he'd been thinking about the way Mack Riley had looked when Rhodes had brought up John West's name. The more he thought about it, the more convinced he was that Riley had been hiding something.

"What is it, then?" Hack asked.

"I wanted you to do something with that computer of yours."

"If you had one in the car, you could do it yourself."

"Not this. I want you to search some records. Can you do that?"

Hack looked offended. "I've done it plenty of times."

"What I'm looking for might never have gone to court."

"If a complaint was filed, it's in there. The courthouse is up to date, even if the sheriff's office isn't. What was it you wanted to know about?"

"I want to know if there's ever been trouble between Mack Riley and John West."

"You don't think Mack killed anybody, do you?"

"I don't know. I just think there was something between him and West that he doesn't want me to know about."

"Well, if there was, I can find it," Hack said, turning to his computer. "You just give me a few minutes."

Rhodes went over to his desk to write up a report

on his response to The County Line call. He was still working on it when Hack said, "Here it is."

Rhodes took off his glasses and put them in his pocket.

"Tell me about it," he said.

TWENTY-SEVEN

WHAT HACK HAD FOUND was a record of a complaint filed against John West by Mack Riley. It had been filed three years earlier, and in the complaint Riley alleged that West had assaulted him.

"Never went to court," Hack said. "Mack dropped the charges."

"Why did West assault him?" Rhodes asked.

"That's not in here. Just the record of the complaint."

"Computers can't do everything, then, can they."

"They can jab a fella's memory," Hack said. "I know Mack a little, and I heard somethin' about this little argument."

"Tell me, then."

"Well, as best I remember it, West owed Riley some money, maybe a good bit. When Riley tried to collect, West threw him out."

"Why didn't it go to court, then?"

"I don't know about that, but usually it's because the money gets paid. That generally settles things pretty quick."

"Why would West owe Mack Riley money?"

"I don't know," Hack said. "I can guess, though."

Rhodes waited. Hack turned back to the TV set. After a minute or so Rhodes gave up.

"Tell me what you'd guess, then."

Hack looked up from the TV. "Well, you might not know this, but old Mack's made a lot of money over the years one way or another."

"I knew he had some money," Rhodes said. "I don't know how he got it."

"Speculatin'," Hack said. "Sometimes when people default on a mortgage, he'll buy the house from the bank. It's usually in pretty bad shape, so he gets it fixed up cheap and sells it for a profit."

Rhodes remembered what Riley had said about dealing with painters and Mr. Fix-its. It hadn't registered at the time, but now Rhodes knew what Riley had meant.

"And you think he did that with John West's house?" he asked Hack.

"He might have," Hack said. "And if West got behind in the payments, that could've caused the trouble."

It was too late to talk to anyone who kept normal Clearview hours, so Rhodes didn't think it would be a good idea to talk to Kara West until the next day. The County Line might be going strong, but there were still a lot of people who watched the ten o'clock news and then went straight to bed. The news had been over for a while, but that was all right. The going to bed part was still a good idea. Rhodes told Hack good night and went home.

IVY WAS SITTING UP in bed reading, her back braced by a thick triangular pillow.

"What's the name of the book?" Rhodes asked.

"Voodoo River," Ivy said. "It's about a private detective named Elvis."

"Good name. Can he sing?"

Ivy put a piece of paper in the book to mark her place, closed the book, and laid it on her nightstand.

"I don't know. It doesn't say. He gets very emotional, though. Why is it that you never seem to get emotional about your work?"

"You know us Texas men. We don't like to show our feelings."

"That's what you'd like for people to think. If you'll go take a shower, I can get you to show a feeling or two."

"You really think so?"

Ivy smiled and nodded. "I'd be willing to bet on it."

Rhodes smiled, too. "Sounds like a pretty safe bet to me," he said.

SUNDAY MORNING was cold and dry. The wind had died down to nothing, and there were no clouds at all. Speedo loved it. He rollicked all around the yard, tossing his frog into the air. Rhodes didn't have time to play with him for more than a minute or so, but Speedo didn't seem to mind. He was having plenty of fun all by himself.

Which was just as well, since Rhodes didn't think this would be a good time to introduce Yancey. The Pomeranian was curled up on his tattered towel, awake but not yet ready to venture out into strange new surroundings.

Rhodes drove by the jail and checked in with

Hack. There were no special problems to deal with, so he went to pay a call on Kara West. It was a little before nine o'clock when he got to her home, but she didn't look as if she was dressed for housework. She was wearing a dress, her hair was done and her makeup was perfect.

"Were you going to church?" Rhodes asked. "I won't keep you long."

"I wasn't going to church this morning. With John gone, I just feel better when I'm dressed up a little. I'll be starting to work at the store in a few more days. I'm going to learn the business from the ground up. But right now I'm still trying to get adjusted."

She invited Rhodes in and offered him coffee, which Rhodes declined. He never drank coffee, preferring to get his caffeine in Dr Pepper. They sat at the kitchen table, and she drank her coffee from a china cup while Rhodes talked. He noticed her braces again and wondered if they were uncomfortable, but he didn't ask.

What he asked was about West's run-in with Mack Riley.

"That was a long time ago," she said. "The business hit a bad patch, and we had to miss a payment on the house. Mr. Riley came by, and he was a little upset about his money. John didn't blame him. He said he'd try to get it soon."

"I heard there was a fight. Mr. Riley filed assault charges."

Mrs. West took a delicate sip of coffee. "There wasn't any fight, really. Mr. Riley said that John knocked him down, but John just bumped into him. It didn't amount to anything. Mr. Riley filed those charges because he was mad about the money, but he dropped them when we made the payment. We never had to miss again."

"Mack's a little touchy, all right. I'm going to have a talk with him today, myself. Do you think he could still be bitter about the misunderstanding?"

"I don't see how. It was a long time ago. Mr. Riley and John got along fine after that."

"What about Pep Yeldell?" Rhodes asked. "Do you remember telling me that you'd never heard of him?"

Mrs. West's hand shook slightly as she set her cup in the saucer with an audible *clink*.

"Yes," she said. "I never did, until he died."

"I've found out that your husband knew him fairly well. They seem to have spent some time together."

"I didn't know John's friends."

"You told me that," Rhodes said. "I guess you weren't aware that John knew Randall Overton, too."

"Wasn't he the other man who died by accident?"

"That's the one. Did you know him?"

"No. I just heard that he burned to death."

"I think there's some connection among all three deaths, and I'm trying to find it. Who did you say told you that John was seeing other women?"

Mrs. West picked up the coffee cup and looked at Rhodes over the rim. Then she took a sip and put the cup back on its saucer. Her hand wasn't shaking this time.

"I don't believe I said."

Rhodes had known that. He said, "That's right. You just told me that it was someone from the church. I think it would be a good idea if you told me who. It might help."

"I can't remember. If it would help, I'd tell you, but I just don't recall."

She sounded so sincere that Rhodes almost believed her.

MACK RILEY wasn't at home, so Rhodes decided to check out another little theory he'd developed. He drove out to the Old Settlers' Grounds and parked his car. Then he walked down to the swimming pools. The water was calm but covered with leaves that the norther had blown into the pools. Rhodes looked up in the pecan trees, squinting his eyes against the bright sun as he tried to locate the place where the limb had broken off.

It was still and quiet under the trees. Rhodes heard a car somewhere on the road, and then there was silence except for a squirrel chattering in a tree.

Rhodes couldn't spot the squirrel, but it didn't take him long to locate the place where the limb had been. The more he looked at it, the more unlikely it seemed to him that anyone would tie a rope there. The limb hadn't been in the best position for swinging out over the water, and there was a perfectly healthy limb not far away that would have served better.

There had been a period in Rhodes's life when he spent a lot of time in trees. He and the other kids in his neighborhood had climbed trees all the time, seeing who could go the highest and sometimes staying up on their favorite perches for hours.

Climbing had seemed perfectly natural to Rhodes then. He could jump up, grab the lowest limb of a tree, and haul himself right onto it. From there he could go on up, from one limb to the next, as if it were the most natural thing in the world. His mother had called him a little monkey, a name that didn't bother him at all.

That had been so long ago that it was mostly a dim memory now. Rhodes had been in a few trees since, but generally only out of urgent necessity, like the time he'd been trying to escape a killer running the tree whacker that the county highway department used to cut back the branches that hung over the less-traveled roads. That wasn't an experience he wanted to repeat.

He walked over to the pecan tree where he thought the rope had been hanging and reached up. The lowest limb was about a foot above his outstretched hand.

Getting hold of it would have been a cinch for Rhodes when he was a boy, but he'd weighed a lot less then. He'd had more of a vertical leap.

But, still. It was only a foot. Surely he could jump a foot.

Rhodes took off his jacket, wrapped his pistol in it, and laid them on the grass. He measured the distance again with his eyes, crouched down, and jumped for the limb.

His fingers touched it, missed any kind of grip at all, and then his feet jolted against the ground. He didn't remember ever having a jolt like that from such a short drop. Maybe he'd been more shock absorbent as a kid.

He looked up at the limb again. "You can do it," he said aloud, and jumped.

He went barely high enough, and his hands clamped around the limb. For a few seconds he just hung there, dangling with his toes about a foot off the ground. He was pretty sure he couldn't pull himself up the way he'd done when he was a kid, but he gave it a try.

He strained until his face got hot and seemed to swell. His arms tingled, and his palms burned. But he didn't move very far.

He let go of the limb and dropped back to the ground. He was breathing hard, so he sat down for a minute with his back against the tree trunk while he waited for his pulse to slow down. When it had slowed, he took off his shoes and socks, stood up, and jumped again.

He grabbed the limb and started climbing up the trunk of the tree with his feet, moving his hands outward on the limb as he did. After a while he was able to hook his feet around the limb and pull himself up on it.

He had to catch his breath after that, so he sat and looked up at the limbs above him, hoping to find a few that would hold his weight. The bottoms of his feet felt strange, as if they might be scratched, but he didn't try to look at them. He was afraid he might fall if he did.

While he was sitting there, he watched a squirrel jump from one tree to another, grabbing branches that looked as thin as telephone wires. It was moving with a swift confidence that Rhodes envied. When it disappeared from sight, it hadn't slowed down.

"Smart aleck," Rhodes said.

He braced himself against the trunk of the tree and stood up on the limb, surprised to find that his knees were a little unsteady.

He took a deep breath and started to climb.

TWENTY-EIGHT

RHODES STOOD IN THE V formed by a thick branch and the trunk of the tree. He remembered now that one of the best things about climbing trees was how peaceful it seemed up away from the ground. That, and how far you could see.

From where he stood, he could see over the top of the dance pavilion and the persimmon trees near the Burleson cabin and all the way to the county road that skirted the Old Settlers' Grounds. There was a pickup parked on the side of the road, but it was too far away for Rhodes to see if there was anyone in it. Beyond the road he saw white-faced cattle grazing in a field and farther on there was a patch of brown woods.

Practically in front of his eyes was the spiky end of the broken branch, and a foot or so below that, jutting off at a slightly different angle, was the limb that Rhodes would have tied the rope to if he had been the one tying it.

Evidently someone else had thought that limb was better, too. The mark the swinging rope had worn in the branch was plain to see.

Rhodes had suspected something like that might be the case after Ivy had said that the limb didn't have to fall and hit Pep on the head, but he'd had to see for himself. Someone had killed Pep Yeldell, all right.

The way Rhodes figured it, the killer had somehow lured Pep Yeldell to the swimming pool with the intention of doing away with him, maybe by faking a drowning. Rotten limbs fell from trees all the time, but finding one there on the ground was just luck—good luck for the killer, bad luck for Pep. The killer had hit Pep with it, probably knocking him out. That would have made drowning him a lot easier.

After that, the killer—or killers, Rhodes told himself, thinking that there could have been two of them—must have decided to make things look more consistent with the accident idea. To do that, someone would have had to climb the tree. The climb might have been hard in the dark, but Rhodes knew that it wouldn't have been as difficult for a younger person as it had been for him.

Mack Riley didn't exactly fit the profile of a tree climber, but Yvonne Bilson was certainly lithe enough to do it. So was Grat. And when Rhodes thought about it, he couldn't rule Riley out completely. He was pretty agile for an older man.

Rhodes looked down at the river. The turtles were on the log again, or maybe they were different turtles this time. They stayed where they were and enjoyed the sun, completely unaware of Rhodes's presence.

Rhodes was thinking about climbing down when the trunk next to his cheek exploded. The explosion was followed almost instantly by the crack of a rifle, which Rhodes heard but didn't worry about at first because the pain caused by the splinters of wood that stuck in his face was too intense.

A second shot clipped off a small branch just above Rhodes's head. Rhodes froze. He didn't know whether to go up or down or stay right where he was. Blood ran down his cheek and onto his shirt collar.

He was completely defenseless. His pistol was on the ground, wrapped up in his shirt. He could see that the shots were coming from the persimmon trees, but the shooter was too well concealed for Rhodes to get any impression of who it was. It might have been a man or a woman or a goat for all Rhodes could see.

He moved around to the other side of the trunk just before a bullet thunked into the wood where he had been. The trunk saved him that time, but it wasn't going to save him much longer. He was no longer as slender as he had been when he was ten years old and the trunk could have hidden all of him. Besides, the slugs that were slamming into it were big enough to chop it in two if they hit it often enough.

Rhodes thought about the .30-.30 he'd seen in Mack Riley's gun cabinet. It was a powerful gun. Rhodes wondered if he'd live long enough to dig any bullets out of the tree.

A bullet tugged at his shirt, just over one of his love handles. Rhodes put a hand on the spot. There was a tear in his shirt, but no blood. There might be the next time, however, and he knew that he had to do something. He wished he knew what.

One thing was for certain: no one was going to come to his rescue. Out here in the country, rifle shots weren't all that uncommon, even if there was anyone to hear them.

Rhodes looked down at the swimming pool. There was always the chance that he could jump. He wondered how high he was. Thirty feet? Forty? Not that it mattered. If he stayed where he was, he was most likely going to get killed.

Was the pool deep enough for such a high dive, or would he hit the bottom too hard and break a leg? A broken leg wasn't much compared to his life, but what if he hit his head and drowned? Or he might hit his head on a limb on the way down and break his neck.

If any of those things happened, he'd be just another death by accident. It occurred to Rhodes that another death by accident was just what the killer wanted, and he was likely to get it, too.

After all, who was going to climb the tree to look for bullet marks if Rhodes was found lying dead on the ground below? Or drowned in the pool? People might wonder what the sheriff had been doing up in a tree, but it was possible that no one would climb up to see.

Ruth Grady probably would, Rhodes thought. She was thorough, and she would wonder about the splinters in his face.

The thought didn't give Rhodes much comfort. Although the day was cold, he was sweating heavily. He had to make a choice. He could stay in the tree, or he could jump for the water.

He looked down again. There were only a couple of limbs that looked threatening. He might be able to avoid them.

Or he might not.

A bullet whacked into the tree and gouged out a large chunk of wood about six inches from Rhodes's fingers. The idea of losing his fingers chilled him.

The idea of jumping didn't appeal to him much, either. For just the fraction of a second an image of Johnny Weismuller flashed through his mind—Tarzan swinging on a movie jungle vine.

There weren't any vines for Rhodes, but he was able to move himself a little farther out on the branch, far enough, he hoped to avoid hitting the bank.

Another shot cracked the wood near his head. He took a breath and jumped.

TWENTY-NINE

IT HAD BEEN a long time since Rhodes had done a cannonball off the high board at the Clearview swimming pool, but there were some things the body never forgot. He hiked his knees up to his chin, or as close as he could get them these days, and wrapped his arms around his shins.

A limb slapped him in the face as he passed it, driving one of the splinters a little deeper into his cheek. He ignored the pain and tucked his head down to his knees as he tried to concentrate on landing just right.

If he hit just below the base of his spine, he would send water geysering high into the air. He would also be less likely to break any bones than in any other kind of dive.

He didn't have time to think about it much. He hit the water with a tremendous impact and a very satisfying explosion of noise. He was sure that anyone on the bank of the pool would have been drenched. There would have been more enjoyment in the performance if he hadn't struck the water so hard.

And if the water hadn't been so cold. Rhodes hadn't thought it would be so cold. He felt like a block of ice, but not as buoyant.

The water slowed his fall, though not as much as

he would have imagined, and the pool was not as deep as he'd hoped. He plummeted all the way to the bottom, and his tailbone hit the hard concrete with a numbing force that sent a shock wave all the way up his spine.

He writhed around like a stunned octopus, accomplishing about as much as the octopus would have. Several seconds elapsed before he was able to make his legs work, and by that time his lungs were burning and threatening to burst. Just as he thought he might be found lying on the bottom of the pool or floating on top like Pep Yeldell, he managed to plant his feet and shove himself upward.

The way to the top seemed a lot longer than the way down, but he eventually made it, breaking through the surface and sucking in air with great, heaving gasps as frosty drops of water flew from his head.

He didn't have time to enjoy the luxury of being able to breathe, however, because he had to swim for the side. He didn't want to be caught in the middle of the pool if the rifleman came after him.

There was a small chance that the shooter would think he'd hit Rhodes, shot him right out of the tree like a squirrel, or that he'd think Rhodes couldn't survive the fall even if he wasn't shot.

But Rhodes couldn't count on that. He had to consider the strong possibility that the shooter would come to have a look to make sure the job had been done right. And if it hadn't, to finish it.

Rhodes's fingers scraped the bank and he pulled himself out in a rush of water. He tried to stand, fell to his knees, got up into a sort of crouch, and stumbled over to where his jacket lay. He fell down beside it, pulled it to him, and unwrapped the pistol.

There was no one coming that he could see, but he couldn't see very well. Water was running out of his hair and into his eyes. His hearing was of no use to him. He couldn't hear a thing except a high roaring in his ears.

He pulled himself behind the trunk of the tree he had climbed and waited, breathing in huge gulps of air and shivering in his cold, clinging clothes.

Feeling began to return to him slowly. First he realized how cold he was in the shade of the trunk with his clammy wet clothes clutching him and his hair plastered across his forehead. Then he felt the burning in his cheek and put his fingers to the spot where the splinters were. There was no blood, but the spot was very tender.

He waited for a few minutes, until his hand was steady, or nearly steady, and pinched the end of one of the splinters between his thumb and forefinger and pulled it out. It hurt when it slipped from his skin, but not as much as it would have later, when he was feeling things more intensely. He probed until he found another splinter. His fingers slipped off on his first attempt to remove it, and he winced. He got it on the second try.

He sat where he was for about a quarter of an hour. He was still very cold, but the shivering had stopped, and no one came to see if he was dead. Rhodes thought he heard a car start on the road, and he remembered the pickup he'd seen. It was so far away that there was no use in trying to get there before it was gone. He wasn't sure he could walk yet, anyway, much less run.

He waited a few more minutes and then stood up. His knees were a little shaky, but he could walk just fine. He went over to his jacket, picked it up, and put it on. It wasn't much help against the cold that was seeping right down into his bones. He hefted the pistol in his hand. It wouldn't do him any good now, but it was nice to know it was there. He shuddered. He needed to warm up and get dry, but he had to climb the tree again first.

He sighed and took off his jacket. He thought about taking the pistol up the tree with him, but he knew that wouldn't be a good idea. He wrapped it in the jacket again and looked up at the tree. Then he jumped.

It took him three tries to grab the lowest limb, and he thought he wouldn't be able to pull himself up this time, but somehow he did. He climbed up to where he had been before and dug out a bullet with his pocket knife. He started down, glad he didn't have to dive into the pool this time.

As soon as he got in the county car, Rhodes started it, moved the heater lever to Warm, and flipped the fan control to High. The engine was still warm from the trip out of town, and hot air surged out of the vents on the dash and floor. He sat there and let it flow over him.

After a while, when he was feeling almost warm, he got out of the car and walked over to the persimmon trees. He looked around for fifteen minutes, until he was chilled to the bone again, but he found no shell casings. Either the shooter had been calm and careful, or Rhodes had misjudged his position and the shell casings were lying in plain sight somewhere else. Rhodes didn't think that was the case, so he went back to his car and turned on the heater again.

When he was finally feeling warm, he drove back to town.

RHODES WENT HOME and soaked in a tub of hot water. The whole time he was in the tub, Yancey scratched at the bottom of the bathroom door.

Ivy had told Rhodes that she would take the dog for a walk before she left for church, so Yancey didn't want to go outside. He just wanted company. Rhodes didn't. He let Yancey keep on scratching while he thought about who might have been shooting at him.

Mack Riley drove a pickup, but then so did most people in Blacklin County. He wished he'd been more observant, but the pickup had been too far away for him to tell the make. He tried to remember the color, but he couldn't.

He kept turning things over in his mind, trying to remember everything he'd heard and seen in the last few days, sure that there was something he was missing, some connection that was there to be made if only he could make it.

There was no way he was going to make it now. His mind was still in a jumble from his recent experiences.

He closed his eyes and leaned back in the tub, letting the water work on his soreness and trying to relax. The water part worked just fine, but the relaxing was a little harder. He wasn't used to being shot at, and he didn't like it very much. He didn't think he'd like it even if it became a regular thing. In fact, he was sure he wouldn't.

After a while he got out of the tub and dried off. He hadn't made the connection he was searching for, but he figured it would happen sooner or later if it was really there to be made.

Yancey was still scratching on the door, but Rhodes didn't want to have to deal with the dog just yet. He looked at himself in the bathroom mirror. The place on his cheek where the splinters had been didn't look too bad. He could cover it with a square bandage. Maybe Ivy wouldn't notice it.

He found a bandage in the medicine cabinet and tried it. Ivy would notice, all right, but that couldn't be helped.

He'd brought clean clothes into the bathroom, and when he had dressed, he opened the bathroom door. Yancey came bouncing in, barking. He sounded much bigger than he was.

"Maybe I should take you with me for protection," Rhodes said.

Yancey wasn't interested. He shot around the room, sniffing at the baseboard and the bathtub.

"Then again, maybe not," Rhodes said. "Come on."

Yancey ignored him, dashing back into the hallway. Rhodes caught up with him in the kitchen.

"Want to meet your new brother?" Rhodes asked.

Yancey barked, but Rhodes wasn't sure whether it was a yes or a no. He also wasn't sure it would be a good idea to introduce the two dogs to one another. Speedo might mistake Yancey for a new toy and try to toss him around. It wouldn't be a pretty sight.

"I'll introduce you two later," he said. "Right now I have to see a man about a gun."

THIRTY

IT WAS A QUIET Sunday in Clearview, and the streets were practically deserted. That was because it wasn't quite time for church to be over. The Methodists were always the first ones out. They started early and finished around 11:30, a good half hour before the Baptists. The Methodists joked that they liked to get to the restaurants before the Baptists got there and took all the tables. Sometimes Rhodes wasn't so sure it was a joke.

Mack Riley didn't go to church. In fact, Rhodes wasn't even sure he'd been to bed. When he came to the door, he was still wearing the same old bathrobe he'd had on the night before, and he had his copy of *Bleak House* in his hand.

"Good morning, Sheriff," he said. He peered through the screen at Rhodes's face. "What happened to you? Run into a door?"

"More like a tree," Rhodes said, thinking that if Riley had noticed the bandage, Ivy certainly would. "Can I come in for a minute?"

"I was reading this book," Riley said holding it up. "Dickens, remember. I was hoping to have a little time to myself, seeing as how I got interrupted last night and didn't get much reading done."

"It's last night I want to talk about," Rhodes told him. "There were a few things we didn't cover."

"What things?"

"I'd feel better about it if we could sit down," Rhodes said. "I've had a rough morning."

Riley wasn't cordial about it, but he pushed open the screen and told Rhodes to come in. He led the way down the hall to the sitting room.

"You can have that rocker again," he told Rhodes. "I hope this won't take too long."

"It shouldn't," Rhodes said. He glanced over toward the gun cabinet. It didn't look any different. "That's a nice-looking .30-.30 you've got there. Marlin?"

"That's right. Belonged to my daddy. He was a big deer hunter in his later years. I never took to it much, myself."

"Why not?" Rhodes asked.

"I don't have any reason to kill a deer. I don't eat the meat, and I don't want the horns. Why should I go out to a deer stand in the dead of winter and sit there for hours with the freezing wind blowing up my pants legs to shoot an animal that never did anything to me?"

"Good question," Rhodes said. "Mind if I have a look at the gun?"

Riley didn't make any move to get up and open the cabinet. He did put his book down on the floor and rock back and forth in the chair.

"Any special reason you want to see it?" he asked.

"There was something you didn't tell me about last night," Rhodes said. "Something about John West."

Riley slammed his palm on the chair arm. "I knew you'd come back at me on that. I used to have a temper on me, Sheriff, and it got me in trouble a time or two. But I've mellowed down now that I've gotten a few more years on me. That little business with John, that didn't amount to a thing."

"You filed assault charges on him."

"Yeah, I did that, all right. I should've just flattened him."

"What happened?" Rhodes asked.

"It was about a debt he owed me. I went to collect it, and he shoved me around. If I'd been younger, he wouldn't ever have dared it."

"His wife says he bumped you by accident."

"Yeah, she would. She's his wife, isn't she?" Riley caught himself. "Well, she was his wife, until he got himself killed like that. Naturally she'd take his side. That's what wives do."

"He's dead now," Rhodes said. "There's no special need for her to take his side."

Riley didn't agree. "More need than ever, some might say."

Rhodes didn't feel like arguing the point. "What about that rifle? Are you going to give me a look?"

"I don't see why you're so all-fired interested in that gun," Riley said. "It's just an old thirty-thirty. Hasn't been fired in years."

"That's what I'm interested in," Rhodes said. "Somebody took a few shots at me early this morning, and I'd like to rule you out."

Riley practically jumped out of the chair. He

walked over to the gun cabinet, opened the doors, and took out the .30-.30.

Then he turned to face Rhodes and said, "What's to keep me from shooting you right here and now?"

Rhodes forced himself to sit still. "Well, for one thing, Hack knows where I am. You wouldn't want to have Hack on your trail, would you?"

"Hack's older than I am. And he couldn't trail a skunk through a perfume plant."

"You might be underestimating him," Rhodes said.

"Yeah, I might. But I don't think so. I'm not going to shoot you though. It just makes me mad that you think I might, just because I didn't tell you about that little fracas with John West."

"I have to be sure," Rhodes told him.

Riley worked the rifle's lever action a few times to show Rhodes that the gun was empty, then walked over and handed him the rifle.

"Here," he said. "Look it over. You'll see I didn't do any shooting at anybody."

It didn't take much looking. The gun hadn't been cleaned in quite some time. There was dust on the stock and on the barrel, where a couple of tiny dots of rust were showed on the bluing.

"This is a nice gun," Rhodes said. "You ought to take better care of it."

"I know it. But I don't ever think about it. It just sits there in the cabinet, probably hasn't been fired since my daddy died back in 1983."

Rhodes handed him the rifle. "I'm sorry about

having to look, but you did leave out that business with West. And since I'd seen the gun here last night, I thought I'd better check it out."

"I can't say that I blame you. I'd probably do the same thing if it was me. But it sure makes a fella think you don't trust him."

"When it comes to these accidental deaths," Rhodes said, "I don't trust much of anybody."

"I don't blame you for that, either." Riley put the rifle back in the cabinet and closed the doors. "But you ought to think about it from another angle. Maybe those old boys did die by accident. Things like that happen, you know."

Rhodes's hand went to the bandage on his face. "People don't try to kill me because of accidents. There's more to it than that."

"You think somebody's trying to kill you because of the accidents?" Riley asked.

"I can't think of any other reason," Rhodes said.

"You haven't exactly been going around town and making yourself loveable lately. There were quite a few people out there at the Old Settlers' Grounds who didn't like the way you stopped them from moving the Burleson cabin."

"I don't think anybody would shoot me over a thing like that," Rhodes said.

Riley smiled. "I wouldn't be too sure," he said.

THIRTY-ONE

RHODES CALLED HACK on the radio and discovered that nothing much was going on at the jail. Sunday wasn't a big day for crime in Clearview. Rhodes drove by anyway and put the bullet in the evidence locker.

"You want to tell me about that?" Hack asked.

"Not today," Rhodes said. "I'm going on home, and I may not come in this afternoon. You can call me if there's any trouble."

"Don't I always?" Hack asked.

"I guess you do. It's nice to know there's one thing I can count on."

"Well, I'll try not to bother you. You can take a little nap if you want to. You look like you could use it. Prob'ly do you good."

"I'll think about it," Rhodes said.

WHAT HE WAS really thinking about was lunch. It was after one o'clock, and Ivy would be home. Maybe she'd like to go out to eat, if the Baptists hadn't taken all the tables in the restaurants by now. Even if they had, some of the Methodists would be finishing up.

But Ivy had different plans, plans that included fried chicken. Rhodes could smell it when he walked through the back door, and thoughts of mashed potatoes and cream gravy speckled with black pepper filled his head. It had been a long time since he'd had fried chicken for lunch.

He went into the kitchen where Ivy was standing by the stove. She had changed out of her dress into jeans and a shirt, and she was wearing a red apron. The chicken, covered with golden batter, was sizzling in the frying pan. Rhodes's mouth watered.

"What's the occasion?" he asked.

Ivy turned toward him and smiled. "I thought we needed an old-fashioned Sunday dinner for a change. I'm glad you got here in time to enjoy it. I was afraid Yancey and I would have to eat alone."

Yancey was standing not far away, his feet planted firmly on the kitchen floor. He was watching Rhodes as if not quite sure who he was.

"A dog shouldn't eat chicken," Rhodes said. "He might get a bone caught in his throat."

"Grrrrrrrr," Yancey said.

"I think he understood you," Ivy said. "And what happened to your face?"

"I'll tell you about it later," Rhodes said. "Right now you better watch that chicken. I think it's about time to turn it over."

"I'll do the cooking. You just do the eating."

"Yes, ma'am," Rhodes said. "I'm good at that."

AFTER LUNCH, which did indeed include mashed potatoes and cream gravy, Rhodes helped Ivy clear the table and told her about his morning.

"I'm glad you waited until after we had lunch,"

she said, putting a plate into the dishwasher. "I'm not sure I could have eaten if you'd told me earlier."

"It wasn't so bad," Rhodes said.

Ivy sat at the half-cleared table and looked at him. "Yes, it was. It was worse, because you never do tell me how bad things really were. You're a typical man. You minimize things because you're afraid I won't like knowing just how much danger you were in or because you think it's not macho to admit you were scared."

"I was scared," Rhodes said. "I don't mind admitting it."

"It doesn't count to admit it after I've brought it up. Now it sounds almost as if you're joking."

Rhodes thought about the way he'd felt when the first bullet hit the tree, and about the way he'd felt when he'd jumped. About waiting behind the tree, shivering with cold and wondering if the shooter was going to come after him.

"I'm not joking," he said.

Ivy picked up the salt shaker and looked at it as if examining it for cracks. Then she set it back where it had been.

"I know you're not joking," she said finally. "It's just that I don't like it when something like this happens. You're not always going to be so lucky, you know."

"Luck?" Rhodes said. "Who said it was luck? It was skill and science, that's what it was."

"Now you really are joking about it."

"I know it. Sometimes you just have to make

light of things. It's easier to deal with them that way."

"Easier for you, maybe. I don't like it, not even a little bit."

While she was speaking, Yancey, who had gone away for a rest, came back into the room. He looked at Rhodes and bared his tiny teeth. Then he began to growl.

"Are we having a fight?" Rhodes asked.

"Are you talking to me or to Yancey?" Ivy asked.

"You. But I can tell that Yancey's not exactly pleased with me, either."

"And I don't blame him a bit. But we're not having a fight. I told you the other day that I knew what I was getting into when I married you. Maybe I was joking a little bit then about the 'man of action' part, but I didn't think you'd be going around getting shot at and jumping out of trees and going swimming when it's forty degrees outside. Anyway, I know what your job is, and I know you have to do it. But that doesn't mean I have to like it."

Yancey didn't like it either. He was still growling.

"Would it do any good if I promised not to do it again?" Rhodes asked.

"No, because I know good and well you *would* do it again if you had to. And because you can't promise that nobody's going to be shooting at you any more."

"People don't shoot at me *often*," Rhodes said.

"And it's a good thing, too. Yancey and I don't like it."

Yancey continued a low growling, but his teeth were no longer bared. Rhodes took that as a good sign.

"I won't get shot at this afternoon for sure," Rhodes said.

"Why not?"

"Because I'm going to stay at home with you. Maybe we could watch a movie."

"That sounds like a good idea. Popcorn?"

"I'll make it myself."

"Even better. And after the movie?"

"After the movie," Rhodes said, "I'm going to church."

THIRTY-TWO

BROTHER ALTON sat straight in his chair. He was in his Sunday best, which wasn't that much different from his everyday dress. The black suit, in fact, looked almost exactly the same, except that it might have been a little newer. The tie had a slightly different pattern, and the white shirt was cleaner.

"I'm working on my sermon for the evening," he said when Rhodes came into the little office. "I don't have much time to talk."

"This won't take long," Rhodes said. "I'd like to know something about Kara West. She's given quite a bit of money to your church, hasn't she?"

"I don't discuss the giving habits of my members," Brother Alton said. "In fact, I don't really keep up with what an individual gives. I don't want to know things like that."

"Who does keep up with it?" Rhodes asked.

"The church secretary. But that information is confidential."

Rhodes didn't really care. He already knew that Mrs. West had given money to the church. The amount didn't particularly interest him.

"I don't want to know about the money," he said. "What I want to know has more to do with her marriage. And with her husband."

Brother Alton pursed his lips. "I don't gossip about my flock."

"But does your flock gossip about its members?" Rhodes asked.

Brother Alton sat up a little straighter, if that was possible. He obviously didn't like the question.

"I don't know what you mean," he said.

"Mrs. West told me that someone from this church told her that her husband was fooling around with other women."

"The church isn't a place where perfect people come on Sunday to pass judgment on others," Brother Alton said.

Rhodes didn't quite get it. "You want to explain that?"

Brother Alton took off his glasses, closed his eyes, and pinched his nose where the glasses had left little red marks on either side. Then he put the glasses back on and looked at Rhodes as if he were a little dense.

"Church members are as likely to gossip about each other as the unchurched are," Brother Alton said. "But I don't think anyone would have said that about John West."

Rhodes didn't see why not.

"Because," Brother Alton said, "my flock wouldn't know about something like that."

Rhodes must have smiled, because Brother Alton said, "I know what you're thinking. And I know what I just said about church members being as inclined to gossip as anybody. But they wouldn't know about John West fooling around because most of them don't go to places where things like that go on."

"The County Line?" Rhodes said.

The preacher looked at Rhodes as if Rhodes had just blasphemed in the sanctuary.

"I've heard of that place," Brother Alton said. "My members don't go there."

Rhodes wasn't so sure about that, but he said, "All right. But that doesn't mean they couldn't have heard something from someone who did go."

"They might have heard something, but it wouldn't have been the truth. So I doubt that they would have repeated it." He saw Rhodes's look and continued, "Gossip is one thing. Malicious, untrue gossip is something else."

Rhodes thought that Brother Alton was about as expert at splitting hairs as anyone he'd ever talked to.

"How do you know it wouldn't have been true?" he asked.

"Because I knew John West. He was a member of this church, and while he didn't always attend, he was a good man."

"He went to The County Line," Rhodes said. "More than once."

"If that's true," Brother Alton said, "it would only have been within the last year. That's when his attendance started to drop off. His wife never was as regular as he was."

Brother Alton might not be a gossip, but if you kept him talking for a while, sooner or later he'd let something interesting slip out.

Rhodes said, "He came to church alone, then?"

"Most of the time. Except for the last year or so when he barely came at all. But I'm sure he had a good reason."

Probably a hangover, Rhodes thought. He said, "But his wife was never much of a churchgoer?"

"Not that I know about," Brother Alton said.

"I wonder why she's been so generous to you lately, then?" Rhodes said.

"You'd have to ask her about that," Brother Alton told him.

RHODES LEFT THE CHURCH and drove over to the jail. Brother Alton had confirmed what Tuffy West had said some time earlier, that John West wasn't a womanizer. And Yvonne Bilson hadn't mentioned a woman being with West at The County Line.

Rhodes wondered who had told Kara West that her husband was seeing other women, and why. And if it hadn't been someone from the church, why had she lied about it?

Of course the fact that Brother Alton insisted that it hadn't been a church member didn't really mean much. He'd admitted that they gossiped, which was certainly no surprise. And someone who gossips wasn't likely to care very much whether the gossip being passed along was absolutely true, no matter what Brother Alton thought. At any rate, it gave Rhodes one more thing to think about.

HACK AND LAWTON were arguing about Ma and Pa Kettle when Rhodes got to the jail, with Lawton maintaining that there were three Pa Kettles before the series ended. Hack insisted that there had been only two.

"Name 'em, then," Hack said. "Go ahead. If you think there was three of 'em, you try to say who they were. I'll bet you a dollar you can't do it."

"Gamblin's against the law," Lawton said with a glance in Rhodes's direction. "I might get arrested."

"I'll go light on you," Rhodes said, heading for his desk and hoping not to get involved.

"Go on, then," Hack said. "You heard him. He'll prob'ly let you off with just cleanin' the cells good for a change."

"You sayin' I don't clean 'em good now?"

"I'm saying there weren't any three Pa Kettles, and you can't name 'em."

"Well, the best one was Percy Kilbride," Lawton said. "I guess you won't argue about that."

"Course I won't. But that's just one. You still got two more to go."

Lawton lifted his cap and scratched his head. "Well, there was that guy that I always get confused with some other guy."

Hack snorted. "If that's the best you can do, you might's well pay me my dollar right now. I'm gonna get it in the end, anyway."

"Arthur somethin' or other," Lawton said. "Kennedy?"

"I don't know 'bout any Kennedys except Teddy and his brother John F.," Hack said. "You give up?"

Lawton snapped his fingers. "Hunnicutt! Arthur Hunnicutt's who it was."

"That's just two," Hack said.

"Well, there was another one. I just can't think of who it was."

"That's 'cause there wasn't one. Pay up."

Rhodes had his glasses on, and he was shuffling through a stack of reports, trying to look very busy. Lawton sidled up to his desk anyway.

"Sheriff," Lawton said, "you know about old movies and stuff like this. Who was the other one?"

"Wasn't any other one," Hack said.

Rhodes sighed and took off his glasses. He rubbed his nose just like Brother Alton had done, putting it off as long as he could.

Finally he said, "Parker Fennelly."

"There you go," Lawton said. "I knew it. Percy Kilbride, Arthur Hunnicutt, and Parker . . . what'd you say his name was, Sheriff?"

"Fennelly," Rhodes said. "Parker Fennelly."

"Right," Lawton said. "Parker Fennelly. One, two, three. I guess I'll take my dollar now, Mr. Hack."

He was reaching his hand toward Hack when Rhodes said, "But Arthur Hunnicutt didn't play Pa."

"Gotcha!" Hack said, slapping at Lawton's hand. Then he said, "Are you sure about that, Sheriff? I'd hate to have to pay Lawton a dollar, but I thought I saw the one where that Arthur guy was Pa."

"Yeah," Lawton said. "That's for certain. He

was in the one about the moonshiners. It was just the other guy I was worried about thinkin' of.''

"Parker Fennelly," Rhodes said.

"Yeah, that's the one. But Arthur Hunnicutt, that's a seven for sure.''

"Not quite," Rhodes said. "Arthur Hunnicutt played Ma's brother-in-law."

Hack laughed. "That settles it," he said. "You can't beat the sheriff when it comes to that stuff, Lawton. You might as well get that dollar out and hand it to me."

Lawton tugged a worn leather billfold from his back pocket and took out a dollar. He handed it to Hack without another word.

"Look at this dollar," Hack said, holding it up. "Looks like it's been in there since about 1956."

Lawton said, "I think I'll go clean the cells real good."

Rhodes and Hack both laughed, and Rhodes wondered just what there was about the conversation that bothered him.

"Maybe that's it," Rhodes said. "Maybe I just need to relax and forget about it for a few days."

THIRTY-THREE

THERE WAS NO pressing business at the jail, other than settling more arguments about old movies. This time the subject was Francis the Talking Mule and whether Donald O'Connor had been in all the movies. Rhodes didn't want to get into any more of that. He stayed for a few minutes to look over some arrest reports and then drove home.

It was getting late, but there was still a little daylight left, so he and Ivy took Yancey outside to introduce him to Speedo.

Speedo didn't seem impressed. Neither did Yancey. They sniffed each other for a while, though Yancey couldn't really get close to the places he wanted to sniff the most, and after that they went to separate sides of the yard. Speedo seemed interested mainly in guarding his toy frog in case Yancey tried to make off with it.

"I think I'll take Yancey for his walk before it gets dark," Ivy said. "Want to come along?"

"I'm going to go inside and try to think," Rhodes said. "I know there's something I've heard about those accidents that ought to mean something to me, but I don't know what it is."

"I'm not surprised. Getting shot at can take your mind off the less important things."

"Maybe that's it," Rhodes said. "Maybe I just need to relax and forget about it for a few hours."

"I can help," Ivy said. "But not until after I take Yancey for a walk."

"I should never have given you that dog," Rhodes said. "He's going to monopolize your time."

"Jealous?"

"Maybe a little."

"That's good," Ivy said. "I like that in a man."

LATER THAT NIGHT Ivy asked Rhodes if he'd remembered what he'd been trying to recall when they were in the yard.

"No," he said. "It's there, but it just won't come to the front."

"What are you thinking about then?"

"The Edsel," he said.

She punched him lightly in the arm. "That's not very flattering."

"Well, I was thinking about the accidents, too. I was sure all along that they were more than just accidents, and the fact that someone took a few shots at me is pretty good evidence that I was right."

"Or that somebody really doesn't like you very much."

"There's that," Rhodes said. "We could haul in half the county for questioning if that were the case."

"I was only kidding," Ivy said.

"So was I. Sort of."

"Like you were kidding about thinking of the Edsel?"

"I wasn't entirely kidding about that. I still haven't talked to Bull Lowery about Yeldell. He worked for Bull, but from what Ruth Grady tells me, Bull didn't like him. And Bull had some dealings with Overton, too. Overton took him pretty good."

"I don't see what all that has to do with the Edsel."

"Bull runs a body shop. I can go by there tomorrow morning and see what he'd charge me for fixing it up."

"And while you're there you can always get in a few subtle questions about whether he happened to kill Pep Yeldell and Randall Overton."

"Not to mention whether he took a few shots at me today."

"You'd better be pretty subtle when you get to that part," Ivy said. "Do you really think he might be the one?"

"That's what I'm going to try to find out," Rhodes told her.

RHODES WENT BY the jail first thing the next morning. A Pacific front had followed the norther into town, and the beautiful weather of the previous day had deteriorated rapidly. The sky was solid gray from horizon to horizon, and the air was filled with a cold mist. Patchy ground fog swirled around Rhodes's legs when he got out of the car, and the jail looked a little like one of the sets from *Castle of Frankenstein.*

Rhodes went inside and had a few words with Ruth Grady, who was about to go on patrol.

"Tell me again about Bull Lowery," he said.

She repeated what she had told him earlier, and Rhodes listened closely, trying to determine if there was anything he'd missed the first time. There wasn't.

"And you're sure he said Pep abused his wife?"

"I'm sure. I've been thinking about that, too. Since no charges were filed, do you think maybe Bull took it on himself to straighten Pep out?"

"I think it's possible," Rhodes said. "And he might have had it in for Overton, too. That could explain two of the victims, but it doesn't explain West."

"West sold auto parts. Maybe there were some bad business dealings there that we don't know about."

"That could be. I'll see what I can find out."

"I'll tell you one thing," Ruth said. "Bull Lowery could have handled them easily. And I don't mean one at a time. He could have handled all three of them at once."

"He could handle all three of 'em and you could throw in a couple more their size to boot," Hack said. He'd been pretending not to listen to their conversation, but he obviously couldn't resist breaking in. "Bull's got a neck that must go nineteen inches around, and that's when he's been on a diet. I hear he hammers out most of the fender dents with his bare fist."

"Want me to go along for backup?" Ruth asked Rhodes.

"Thanks for the offer," Rhodes said. "But I don't think I'll need any help. If Bull did anything wrong, I'll bring him in myself."

"You're gonna get in trouble with that lone wolf stuff one of these days," Hack said.

Ruth turned to look at him. "*Get* in trouble? Where have you been for the last year or two?"

"I won't get in trouble," Rhodes said.

He didn't think this would be a good time to bring up what had happened to him at the Old Settlers' Grounds. Ruth and Hack might try to make more of it than the situation warranted. Bring Ivy in, and they could have a high old time telling him about his casual disregard for his own health and safety.

"Bull Lowery could break your neck with one hand," Hack said. "Less than that. Two fingers, prob'ly. Wouldn't even work up a sweat while he was at it, either."

"I won't give him the chance," Rhodes said, wondering if he was being foolish.

Hack gave him a gloomy look. "It's times like this I'm glad the county has good insurance on us. They don't have any burial policy, though. You ever thought about getting one?"

"Not lately," Rhodes said. "But I appreciate the vote of confidence."

Hack was shaking his head when Rhodes went out the door.

THIRTY-FOUR

BULL LOWERY'S BODY SHOP was in an old sheet metal building on a side street not far from Clearview's downtown area. The body shop had been there ever since Rhodes could remember. Chub Lowery had run it from the early 1950s until his death, and then his son Bull had taken over.

There was a blue-and-white sign in front, giving the name of the shop and letting everyone know that they could rely on Lowery Paint and Body to give free estimates, not to mention that the establishment would pay $50 of the deductible on all windshield replacements. It still wasn't raining, but the mist and fog had covered the sign with droplets of water that slid down its slick metal surface and dripped off the bottom edge.

Rhodes parked next to a dark green Camaro with a crumpled fender, got out, and went inside. He smelled the sharp odor of fresh paint and saw a Chevy pickup with its glass and chrome protected by paper and tape. It had a fresh coat of shiny blue metallic paint. In the back of the shop someone was banging on metal with a rubber mallet. The noise almost drowned out the chugging of the shop's air compressor.

Lowery's office was in a little room that had been added to the inside of the building. There was a big window through which Rhodes saw Lowery sitting at a desk and talking on an old-fashioned black telephone. Lowery was big, all right, wide and squat and powerful. His neck was just as big as Hack had said it was. He was wearing a black baseball cap turned backwards so that Rhodes couldn't see the emblem on the front.

Lowery looked up and saw Rhodes through the window. He put up a big hand and motioned for Rhodes to come inside the office, so Rhodes opened the door and stepped in.

"Yeah, yeah," Lowery said into the phone.

In spite of Lowery's size, Rhodes had always heard that his voice, not his physique, had given him his nickname. It was a deep croak, and for most of his life he had been known as Bullfrog. In recent years the frog part had been dropped off and the name shortened. Rhodes didn't know why.

"I can get to it tomorrow," he told his caller. "No, fixin' a headliner's no big deal. I do it all the time. The glue gives out in all those GM cars about that age, and the liner just falls right down on your head. Yeah, I know it's a pain. You get it in here about eight o'clock tomorrow, and I'll take care of it. I'll have it out for you by Wednesday."

After the caller agreed to bring in the car, Lowery hung up and looked at Rhodes. "What can I do for you, Sheriff?"

"I wanted to talk to you about your brother-in-law."

"Which one? I got two of them."

"Pep Yeldell."

"Yeldell? He don't count. He's my ex-brother-in-law. And he's dead."

"You don't seem very upset about it."

On Lowery's desk there were an electric adding machine, the telephone, a credit card reader, a thick pad of work-order forms, and an ashtray that held a dead cigar with a wet-looking, well-chewed end. Lowery fished out the cigar and stuck it in his mouth.

"Upset?" he said around the cigar. "Why would I be upset? Hell, I'd dance on his grave if I could dance."

"You told Deputy Grady that Pep abused your sister."

"I didn't say he *abused* her. I said he hit her."

"How often?"

"I can't tell you that because I don't know. But he stopped after I found out about it. I made damn sure he didn't do it again."

That sounded a little ominous to Rhodes. He said, "You want to explain that?"

Lowery chewed his cigar for a second, took it out of his mouth, and set it carefully in the ashtray. The wet end glistened.

"You wouldn't be accusing me of killing the little weasel, would you, Sheriff?" Lowery said.

"You had a motive for it. You had one for killing Randall Overton, too."

"How'd you find out about that business?"

"He kept records."

"Hard to believe he'd have that little sense, him being an out-and-out crook like he was. Anyway what happened with him was my own damn fault. I should've known better than to pay some jake leg like him for a job. I should've known he'd spend the money on women or beer and never do a lick of work. But I took care of him."

Rhodes wished he'd brought a tape recorder. Lowery was practically confessing to doing away with both men.

"What about John West? Did you take care of him, too?"

"John? I didn't have anything against John. We did a little business now and then, but that's about it. He always struck me as being pretty honest."

Oh, well, Rhodes thought. Three confessions in a row would have been too much to hope for.

"Tell me about how you took care of Pep," he said.

"I took him out in back of the shop and beat the tar out of him," Lowery said. "You don't really think I killed him, do you?"

"The thought had entered my mind."

"Well you can get it out of there. I never killed anybody. But as soon as Cissy told me he'd hit her, I taught him a little lesson. When I finished with him, I told him that Cissy would be filing for a divorce and that he'd be moving out. He got out that very afternoon."

"But you kept him on here at the shop?"

"He was good with his hands, and he knew about painting. You didn't have to worry about the paint running or dripping when Pep was doing the job.

Besides, we'd settled our differences, and he wasn't going to be seeing Cissy again.''

"Where were you the night he was killed?"

"I'm glad you asked me that, Sheriff. It just so happens that I was at home with my wife."

Wives could usually be counted on to back up their husbands, and Lowery's probably wasn't any different. Unless she was like Yvonne Bilson.

"Was anybody else with you?" Rhodes asked.

"Sure was. Ken and Verna DuBose. We played Forty-two till about midnight."

Ken DuBose owned the Dairy Queen and had a reputation for honesty. It was a pretty good alibi.

"What about Overton?"

"I asked him for my money back. He got nasty." Lowery made a fist. It was about the size of the old black telephone on his desk. "I clocked him one. He didn't have much to say after that, and I just wrote the money off to experience."

Rhodes was beginning to believe that Lowery was telling the truth. He hadn't been confessing before. He'd just meant that he'd knocked Yeldell and Overton around a little bit.

Rhodes shifted gears. "You told Deputy Grady that no one had brought a Jeep Cherokee in to see about getting any damage repaired."

"Not lately. There's three or four Cherokees around town, but I haven't ever had one of 'em in here." Lowery picked up his cigar, looked at the wet, unappetizing end and set it back down. "I been thinking about that, though."

"Thinking what?" Rhodes asked.

"Pep did a little freelance work, you know?"

"He was a shade-tree mechanic," Rhodes said. "I heard about that."

"Yeah. Well, he did a little body work on the side, too. I wasn't supposed to know about it, since he was cutting me out, but I did. Cissy told me."

Rhodes wondered if that was why Pep had hit her, but he didn't want to get into that.

He said, "She didn't mention a Jeep Cherokee, did she?"

"Nope. But that don't mean there wasn't one. Just suppose old Pep worked on that Cherokee and then decided there might be some more money in it."

"You mean blackmail?" Rhodes said.

"Yeah. It'd be just like the little weasel. You ever think about that?"

Rhodes had thought about it, all right, but not exactly this way.

"Did Pep have the equipment to do the work at home?"

"Nah, probably not. But he had a key to this place. He could've done the work on a Sunday and nobody the wiser unless I just happened to drive by."

"Did you make it a habit to come by on Sunday?"

"I never come by. Pep knew that."

"If Pep worked on it here, what happened to the car?" Rhodes asked.

"Hey," Lowery said. "I can't do all your work for you, can I?"

"I guess not." Rhodes said, and it suddenly occurred to him that he might already know the answer to his question. However, he had something else to talk to Lowery about, so he said, ''I might have a little body work for you, myself.''

''Yeah? What kind?''

''I bought an Edsel,'' Rhodes told him.

''Not that one in Overton's driveway.''

''That's the one.''

''Well, I won't ask you what you paid for it, but you probably got a good deal. The body was in pretty good shape. You'll be needing some upholstery, a paint job, maybe some chrome and a little body work. I don't know about the taillights. Those get broken pretty often. Parts are gonna be hard to come by, but you can get 'em. You could check with Tuffy West about that. He's got a computer that's in touch with junkyards all over the country.''

Computers again, Rhodes thought. Hack would be proud.

''If a part's out there,'' Lowery went on, ''Tuffy can get it for you. I tell you what, you bring that car in, and I'll give you a free estimate. You won't find a better price in town, either. I can promise you that. What I can't promise you is whether it'll run. I don't do mechanic work.''

''But you can take care of everything else.''

''That's right. It'd be a pleasure to work on that ugly old car. You just leave it to me.''

Rhodes said that he'd probably do that.

THIRTY-FIVE

RHODES WAS ON HIS WAY to Tuffy West's junkyard when Hack called on the radio.

"Ivy wants you to phone her," he said. "She says you've been holding out on her."

"Holding out about what?" Rhodes asked.

"She didn't tell me that. I'm just the old dispatcher. Nobody ever tells me anything."

Rhodes could tell from Hack's tone that the dispatcher's feelings were hurt, and he thought he could guess the reason why.

"Ivy told you about me getting shot at, didn't she," Rhodes said.

"I ain't sayin' she did, and I ain't sayin' she didn't. Course, it'd be your place to tell me about somethin' like that. If you wanted me to know about it, that is."

"I didn't feel like talking about it."

"That's just fine with me. It ain't none of my business. If you want to keep ever'thing a secret, you just keep it a secret. It's all the same to me."

"I'll tell you about it later," Rhodes said.

"Can if you want to. Don't have to, though. I wouldn't want you to put yourself out any."

"Did Ivy say where she was?"

"She's at work. You got the number?"

"I know what it is," Rhodes said.

RHODES STOPPED AT a pay phone and called Ivy.

"Why didn't you tell me about Kara West's makeover?" Ivy asked.

"I guess I forgot," Rhodes said, wondering why Ivy cared. He hoped she wasn't thinking about coloring her hair. "Where did you hear about it?"

"At the Hair Barn. That's where I get all the news."

The Hair Barn was the shop where Ivy got her hair washed, cut, and blown dry. Rhodes had never understood the appeal of the name. It sounded to him like the name of a place where hair was stored in bales, like hay. But the name aside, Ivy was right about one thing: If you wanted the news—the *real* news—about Clearview, the Hair Barn was a more reliable source than either the newspaper or the radio station.

"I forgot this was haircut day. Are you thinking about getting braces? You sure don't need them."

"I'm not thinking about anything like that. I'm thinking about why Kara West got a makeover."

"Her husband just died. She probably wanted to do something to make herself feel better."

"Maybe. But I think a woman usually does something like that for other reasons."

"What other reasons?"

"A man," Ivy said.

"I never thought about that," Rhodes admitted. "She seemed genuinely sad that John was dead. I felt sorry for her. I thought she was just trying to make herself feel better."

"You can be sad even if you have somebody else

lined up," Ivy told him. "And you can get a make-over for another man as well as for yourself."

Rhodes could feel his clothes soaking up the damp cold. He rubbed his hand across his face and wiped the moisture on his jacket.

"That's a comforting thought," he said.

"I'm not trying to comfort you. I'm just saying that it might throw a new light on those accidents of yours."

"Kara West couldn't have killed those three men," Rhodes said. "She might have run over John, but she wasn't strong enough to have killed Pep."

"How strong do you have to be to hit somebody in the head with a tree limb?"

Rhodes thought about that for a second. "Good question," he said.

RHODES DROVE out of town to Tuffy West's wrecking yard. The wide front gate was open, and Rhodes could see the tangle of old cars that the fence was supposed to hide. Tuffy hadn't gone to the expense of paving the entrance, or any of the rest of the yard for that matter, so the county car splashed through wide, dark puddles as Rhodes drove inside.

Rhodes parked beside Tuffy's wrecker and went inside the building. Tuffy was inside behind the high counter watching a little TV like the one Hack had at the jail. He had it turned up loud, and Rhodes could hear Rod Roddy yelling for someone to "Come on down." Rhodes had heard that Roddy was from Ft. Worth originally, but he didn't know whether that was true.

Tuffy looked up from the TV when Rhodes walked across the oily concrete floor to the counter. When he saw who his visitor was, he turned off *The Price Is Right* and smiled.

"You caught the bastard that killed my brother yet?" he asked.

"Not yet," Rhodes said. "But I'm working on it."

"Good. What can I do for you, then?"

"I bought an Edsel," Rhodes told him. "I was wondering how hard it would be to get parts for it."

"An Edsel, huh? Well, it won't be easy gettin' parts for her, I can tell you that. Not as hard as you might think, though. Most of the parts are interchangeable with parts from old Fords and Mercurys. Those old Edsels are mighty popular with collectors right now. I don't know why 'cause they're so ugly—sorry if that hurts your feelin's, Sheriff, but they are."

Rhodes didn't care what Tuffy West thought about the Edsel's appearance. He just wanted to know about the parts.

"I got me a computer, and I'm in touch with places all over the U. S. A.," Tuffy continued. "So if the parts are out there, I can find 'em for you."

"I don't know what I'll need yet," Rhodes said. "I haven't really looked at the car very carefully."

"Is it that one Randy Overton had?"

"That's the one."

"It was in pretty good shape. His daddy took care of it, and it's been under that tarp ever since."

"You called him Randy," Rhodes said. "Were you two pretty good friends?"

Tuffy narrowed his eyes. "I knew him. Lots of people knew Randy."

"But how many people knew Overton, Yeldell, and John West?" Rhodes asked.

"Plenty, I bet. Why? What difference does it make?"

"It wouldn't make any difference if they hadn't all been killed," Rhodes said.

Tuffy shrugged. "Accidents happen."

"Sure they do. But your brother wasn't an accident."

"I wasn't talkin' about John. I was talkin' about the other two."

"Those weren't accidents," Rhodes said.

"Yeah? What makes you think so?"

"Somebody killed them," Rhodes said. "Somebody who knew all three of them. Somebody who's lied to me about them two or three times already."

"You better not be talkin' about me," Tuffy said.

"I am, though," Rhodes said.

Rhodes had thought about things for a long time after hanging up the pay phone. He'd stood out in the weather until his pants legs were wet and sticking to him the way they had when he'd climbed out of the pool at the Old Settlers' Grounds.

Eventually he'd gone over everything that people had said to him, and he'd realized that Tuffy had been lying right from the start.

It was the brother-in-law business from the Ma and Pa Kettle debate that had bothered Rhodes.

Tuffy was Kara West's brother-in-law, the one on whose shoulder she'd been crying so hard at the funeral. Rhodes should have been suspicious then. He should have known it was Tuffy all along.

"You told me that John left The County Line alone," Rhodes said. "But he didn't. He left with you."

"Who says?" Tuffy asked through clenched teeth.

"That doesn't matter," Rhodes said, hoping that Yvonne Bilson would be willing to testify in court. "You also told me that you didn't remember whether you saw Pep that night. But according to my witness, you did see him."

"That's a lie," Tuffy said.

"We'll have to let a jury decide that," Rhodes said. "Besides, there's more."

"There can't be."

"There's Pep. Did you let him have a look at John's Cherokee to see if he could fix it? It might have brought more if you sold it in Mexico or somewhere than if you just broke it down for parts."

"I don't know what you're talking about."

"Then why did you take those shots at me yesterday?"

Tuffy tried to look surprised. He wasn't very good at it, and his voice rose a little.

"Me?" he asked.

"You," Rhodes said. "I figure Mrs. West called you right after I left her house. She must have told you I knew about Pep and John being friends. You were probably already planning to come over. She was dressed for a visitor, and I wasn't the one she was expecting.''

Tuffy opened his mouth as if he were going to say something, maybe deny something. But no words came out.

Rhodes waited for a second, then said, ''You must have gone over to Mack Riley's looking for me. I told Mrs. West that's where I was headed. Maybe you were planning another little accident for me, maybe not. But you got your chance when I went to the Old Settlers' Grounds.''

''That's a bunch of crap.'' Tuffy was no better at sounding convincing than he was at sounding surprised. But he kept trying. ''I never did anything.''

''I have a slug from the rifle that fired the shots,'' Rhodes said. ''I'll just have to match them to your thirty-thirty to prove that you're the one.''

''I don't have a thirty-thirty.''

''Maybe not. But I'd say the slug was about that size. Maybe it wasn't. What kind of rifle do you have, anyway?''

''This kind right here,'' Tuffy said, ducking down behind the counter and coming up with a rifle that he stuck right in Rhodes's face.

THIRTY-SIX

RHODES BARELY HAD TIME to jerk his head to the side before Tuffy fired. Flame burned Rhodes's eyes as the bullet zipped by him and into the stack of tires on the opposite wall. Rhodes hit the floor and rolled.

Tuffy climbed up on the counter and worked the rifle's lever action. A brass shell winked in the air, and Tuffy aimed the rifle as Rhodes tried to stand and reach his pistol. He didn't get his hand on it because his foot slipped in a patch of oil. He fell again, which might have been the reason that Tuffy's next shot missed. The bullet sparked off the concrete floor and whined into the tires.

Rhodes came up on his hands and knees, still trying to get his pistol out.

Tuffy didn't want him to get it. He was clearly beyond caring about whether Rhodes's death appeared to be an accident. He fired his rifle again.

Rhodes dived to his left, hit on his shoulder, and rolled under the same car that had been there on his last visit. The engine was still hoisted out, hanging above the empty engine compartment on a thick chain.

It didn't hang for long. Tuffy ran to the hoist and released the catch. There was a high-pitched squeal, the chain rattled, and the engine fell.

Rhodes was already slithering out from under the other side of the car when the engine struck the concrete with the sound of one boulder ramming another.

Tuffy cursed. It would have been hard to explain just why Rhodes was under the car, but Tuffy could have come up with something. Rhodes could practically hear him.

"God knows why that hoist let go. The Sheriff was under there checking out something he wanted to see for that old Edsel he bought, and the chain must've slipped. Maybe the catch was defective. You could check it out."

And of course by then the catch would be defective. Tuffy would make sure of that. Rhodes crouched beside the car, his pistol now in his hand, waiting for Tuffy's next move.

It was very quiet, and Rhodes could hear the rain, falling harder now, drumming on the tin roof of the building. Then Rhodes heard Tuffy starting the wrecker.

Rhodes jumped up and ran around the car. When he got to the door, Tuffy leaned out of the wrecker and fired two rounds. Rhodes heard something buzz just over his head, and Tuffy ducked back into the wrecker.

Rhodes stopped and brought his pistol up in a two-handed grip. He fired twice, starring the wrecker's windshield at just about the level of Tuffy's head. Tuffy had ducked out of the way, but the wrecker choked and died.

Rather than trying to start it again, Tuffy bailed

out of the wrecker door and ran across the parking area, carrying the rifle in his right hand.

Rhodes went after him, splashing through the cold puddles. If Tuffy got into the maze of old automobile bodies, he was going to be hard to find, but there was no way to stop him short of shooting him.

And there wasn't much chance of shooting him. A running man with adrenaline pumping through him might be able to hit something the size of an elephant, but anything smaller was just about impossible.

The rain began to fall even harder, throwing a gray curtain over the wrecking yard. Rhodes could hardly see the junked cars as he ran past them, their hoods wide open like the mouths of giant metal birds in a weedy nest.

Tuffy ducked down a row where cars were stacked on top of one another two and three high, and Rhodes slowed down. He was pretty sure that Tuffy wouldn't just keep running. Sooner or later he was going to stop and make a stand and take a few more shots.

Rhodes tried to think how many times Tuffy had fired the rifle already. Three inside and twice outside, he thought. If the rifle held six rounds like Mack Riley's Marlin, Tuffy had one left. Rhodes didn't think Tuffy would have any extra rounds in his pockets, though he couldn't be absolutely sure. So there would be only one more shot.

Of course one could be enough.

Rhodes stopped beside the shell of an old white Plymouth with a vinyl-covered roof. Atop it there was a fairly new maroon Ford Crown Victoria that had been in a pretty bad accident. The front end was crumpled almost all the way back to the driver's compartment, the seats were missing, the wheels were gone, and the trunk was popped open.

A wrecking yard was the obvious place to hide a Jeep Cherokee, Rhodes thought, and he wondered if John West's Cherokee was somewhere nearby or whether it had been flattened and hauled away. He hoped it was there. It would make his case against Tuffy that much stronger.

Rhodes risked a quick look around the side of the Plymouth. He didn't think Tuffy would shoot on impulse, not if he had only one shot left.

Rain spattered down on the narrow lane between the rows of ruined cars. Green weeds grew thick and tall along the edges of the lane and among the cars. There was no sign of Tuffy.

The smart thing to do, Rhodes knew, would be to go back to his car and have Hack call Ruth for backup. But that would mean leaving Tuffy alone and maybe giving him time to get out of the yard. Rhodes didn't want that to happen.

Sticking close to the car bodies, Rhodes began walking slowly down the right-hand side of the lane. The rain ran down the collar of his jacket and drew chill lines down his back. The weeds brushed against the bottoms of his pants and shed moisture on them. Rhodes wondered if you could really catch pneumonia from getting wet and cold. If you could, he was doomed.

After he had gone a few yards, he could see the

rusty metal fence that bounded the wrecking yard. The cars at the end of the row were practically touching it. If Tuffy climbed on top of the cars, he could jump over the fence. He might already have done it.

Or he might have moved on to another row entirely. Rhodes really had no idea.

Something made a scraping sound just above Rhodes's head, and Rhodes looked up. The body of an old black Chevy sat on top of two other cars, and it moved as Rhodes watched. Then metal screamed, and the body of the Chevy tilted over and fell toward him.

Rhodes threw himself to the side and almost managed to get out of the way. But he didn't quite make it.

The side of the car hit Rhodes in the back and knocked him sprawling. Sparks flashed in front of his eyes, and he thought for just a second that he had lost his grip on the pistol. But he hadn't. It was there in his hand, and he tried to roll over and meet the attack that he was sure was coming. He didn't want to be shot in the back.

Tuffy was still saving his last shot, however. He was running for the fence, jumping from rain-slicked car top to car top. Rhodes tried to sit up, but pain shot up his backbone, and he lay back down. He raised the pistol, but he didn't think he could hit Tuffy.

He didn't have to. Tuffy got almost to the fence, but then his right foot slipped out from under him. He looked almost comical as he rose in the air and landed on his back with a loud thud that dented the car top. The rifle slipped from his fingers and fell to the ground. For just a moment Tuffy lay still. Then he slid slowly off the top of the car. When he hit the ground, the weeds hid him.

Rhodes tried again to sit up. The pain in his back hadn't subsided, but he was able to raise himself to a crouch. He put down a hand and pushed upward. His knees popped, and he thought his back might lock up on him, but it didn't. He straightened as much as he could and took a step.

When his foot touched the ground, an electric shock tingled upward and spread out between his shoulders. Rhodes took another step anyway. It didn't hurt any more than the first one had. It didn't hurt any less, either.

He walked slowly toward where Tuffy had fallen, each step sending a message up Rhodes's back. The message said: "Stop and sit down."

Rhodes was too cold and wet to sit down, and besides, he had to check on Tuffy, who seemed pretty sure to be hurt worse than Rhodes was. Just in case Tuffy was playing possum, however, Rhodes held the pistol ready.

"Tuffy?" Rhodes said when he got near the spot where West had fallen.

There was no answer. Rain beat on the tops of the cars. Rhodes waited, and finally the weeds shook as if someone were moving in them.

"I have you covered, Tuffy," Rhodes said. "And you just have one shot left. You might as well come with me."

"You can go to hell, Sheriff," Tuffy said.

The tip of his rifle poked out from the weeds, and he fired his last shot.

This time, he didn't miss.

THIRTY-SEVEN

RHODES FELT the bullet burn him somewhere high on his shoulder. He sat down, hard. Water splashed around him, and his backbone twanged.

Tuffy came out of the weeds and headed for the fence. Rhodes watched him go and tried to bring up the pistol for a shot. For some reason, he couldn't make his hand move.

When Tuffy reached the last stack of cars, he climbed from bumper to bumper to the top and got ready to jump the fence.

"You'll break your neck," Rhodes called.

Tuffy stopped and looked back. "You could be right, Sheriff. I don't know why I didn't think of that."

He climbed back down and walked toward Rhodes. Rhodes watched him coming through the rain.

"I don't have to jump any fence," Tuffy said. "And I don't have to run. I can just drive the wrecker. Or your car. You'll give me the keys, right?"

"I don't think so. I'll give you a ride to the jail, though."

Tuffy stopped in front of Rhodes and laughed. He wiped the rain out of his face.

"I don't think you're going to take me anywhere,

Sheriff," he said. "You would've shot me by now if you could, so when you give me your keys, you might as well give me the pistol, too."

Tuffy bent down to take the pistol from Rhodes's right hand. Rhodes waited until Tuffy's fingers touched the gun, and then he hit him, bringing his left fist up from the ground with all the strength he had left.

He caught Tuffy right on the point of the chin. Tuffy's teeth clicked together and his head snapped back. Rhodes hit him again before he could fall, catching him on the side of the head this time. There was a loud *pop*, which Rhodes knew was probably his knuckle, though he hoped it was Tuffy's skull, and Tuffy collapsed across Rhodes's lap.

Rhodes let him lie there for a second, then pushed him off. He took the pistol in his left hand and prodded Tuffy hard in the ribs. Tuffy didn't move, but Rhodes felt like hitting him again anyway, maybe in the head, just for fun, but with the pistol this time. He didn't, though, because there was no use in blaming Tuffy for Rhodes's own stupidity. He should have known Tuffy would shoot. It was either that or give up. Rhodes had thought Tuffy would give up, but he'd misjudged him.

Rhodes twisted his neck and tried to see where he'd been shot. He couldn't see the spot, but he didn't think he was hurt badly. He was bleeding, but not much, and he figured the bullet had just creased him. It had taken a little chunk of muscle, however, and Rhodes's shoulder felt as if a Boy Scout had built a fire in it.

After a while Rhodes stood up. It was harder to do than the last time he'd done it, and he swayed for a second after he got to his feet, but he didn't fall back down.

Tuffy was still lying where Rhodes had shoved him, his mouth almost in a puddle that the raindrops dimpled as they fell. Rhodes toed Tuffy's head a little to one side. Tuffy was going to have to lie there until Rhodes could get help, and Rhodes wouldn't want him to drown.

Working mostly with his left hand, which was beginning to swell, Rhodes got Tuffy's hands together behind his back and cuffed them. Tuffy would still be able to walk if he came to, but he wouldn't be driving anywhere or climbing any fences.

Rhodes started back to his car. When he was half-way down the lane, he heard Tuffy calling him.

"You can't leave me here," Tuffy yelled. "I'll get pneumonia."

"Welcome to the club," Rhodes said, and sneezed.

"I'VE NEVER BEEN shot before," Rhodes told Ivy.

"That's pretty lame," she said. "I hope you don't think that excuses you."

They were sitting on the sofa, watching Doris Day and Rod Taylor in *The Glass Bottom Boat*. Rhodes thought Taylor was all right, but he was no Rock Hudson. Of course it could be that Rhodes's judgment was clouded by the time-released decongestant he was taking for his runny nose.

"I didn't mean to get shot," Rhodes said.

"You didn't mean to get shot? That's even worse than saying you've never been shot before. And what about your face? Not to mention your hand."

She touched his swollen hand gently, but it was clear that she was still upset. Rhodes didn't really blame her. He shouldn't have gone to Tuffy's place alone, even if his suspicions hadn't completely hardened, and he'd underestimated Tuffy's ruthlessness.

"Would it help if I said I'm sorry?"

"Maybe."

"I'm sorry."

"That's better. Now say you won't do it again."

"I won't do it again."

"All right. I'll take your word for it. This time. But you'd better not mess up again, Bub."

"Bub?"

"You heard me."

A commercial for a finance company came on, and Ivy reached for the remote to mute the TV.

"You never did say whether Kara West knew what was going on," she said.

Rhodes leaned back on the sofa. "Tuffy says everything was his idea, and I more or less believe him. He fell for Kara, and he thought he could get John out of the way by lying about him. He told Mrs. West that John was going out with other women, but it was just Tuffy he was out with."

"And because Kara trusted her husband, that didn't work," Ivy said, as if she weren't sure that trusting a husband was a wise move.

"It didn't work," Rhodes said. "Not soon

enough to suit Tuffy, anyway. It might have worked, eventually, but Tuffy got in a hurry. Maybe the insurance money had something to do with it, too. John had a good policy, and Tuffy must have thought he could get Mrs. West and the money, too. All he had to do was kill his brother.''

"Brotherly rivalry," Ivy said. "An old story."

"Practically the oldest," Rhodes agreed. "Anyway, he got John drunk, took him out on that road, and told him they were out of gas. John was supposed to walk to town and get some while Tuffy stayed with the car."

"And Tuffy ran over him."

"Well, he didn't run over him. He just hit him."

"Same thing."

"I guess so," Rhodes said. "Pep found out about it because he knew John and Tuffy were together that night and got suspicious. He slipped into the wrecking yard and found West's Cherokee. I thought maybe Tuffy had asked him to repair it, but Tuffy wasn't quite that stupid."

"He wasn't stupid at all. He managed to kill Pep and Randall Overton, didn't he?"

Rhodes nodded.

"But why?" Ivy asked.

"Tuffy says that they were trying to blackmail him. Pep must have told Overton that Tuffy had killed his brother, and the two of them cooked up a scheme to make a little money out of it. That's just the kind of guys they were. They threatened to tell me the story, but I'm sure they didn't care about seeing Tuffy get what he deserved. They thought it was just another scam, another way to make a few easy dollars. But they misjudged Tuffy.'' He paused and looked at Ivy. "Like I did."

"You certainly did," Ivy said. "But you won't do it again. You promised."

"That's right." Rhodes reached for the remote. "Show's coming back on."

Before Rhodes could punch the mute button, Ivy grabbed the remote from him and set it on the coffee table.

She said, "He made all three deaths look like accidents. Not just anybody would have seen the connection."

"Maybe not," Rhodes said. "But there just aren't that many accidents around here. Not fatal ones."

"Don't try to make light of it. You're the one who saw what was going on when no one else did. How'd he kill them, anyway?"

"He got them drunk. It worked on John, and it worked on both of them. Get a man drunk, and you can talk him into a lot of things. Going for a swim, for one. Sitting in the car for a smoke, for another. And then you just take advantage of the situation."

"So they were the stupid ones, not Tuffy."

"Looks that way," Rhodes said.

"What about the Edsel?" Ivy asked.

"We'll just have to hope somebody takes over the wrecking yard. Or we can go somewhere else and try to get parts. Bull Lowery can do the body work, though."

Yancey came bouncing into the room, barking.

"He sure has a lot of energy for such a little dog," Rhodes said.

"He's hungry, and someone should take him for a walk," Ivy told him.

Rhodes reached to the bandage that wrapped his shoulder and moaned loudly.

"I'd do it," he said, "but I've been shot."

"I'll do it then," Ivy said. "Does your arm really hurt under that bandage?"

"Yes. It itches, too."

"Good," Ivy said. She punched the mute button, and the sound came back on.

EDGAR AWARD WINNER
MICHAEL JAHN
MURDER ON THEATRE ROW

A CAPTAIN
BILL DONOVAN MYSTERY

The historic Knickerbocker Theatre is about to reopen
with a star-studded musical extravaganza—but murder
threatens to derail the show. The list of suspects is long,
but the most illogical one is Milos the Magnificent, long
dead and buried in the basement of the theater. Bodies are
falling faster than the curtain on a bad production.

Operating with the logic that ghosts don't commit
murder, Captain Bill Donovan searches for a killer who's
prepared to bring down the house with his own carefully
orchestrated production: death, the musical.

Available April 2000 at your favorite retail outlet.